ALSO BY KIMBERLY JONES & GILLY SEGAL

I'm Not Dying with You Tonight

A NOTE FROM
THE AUTHORS

Like our first coauthored novel, *Why We Fly* was inspired by real events. In late 2016, a number of athletes took a knee during the playing of the national anthem to protest racial injustice and police brutality. Colin Kaepernick was among the earliest activists to take this action, though he was soon joined by others, including the players of the Women's National Basketball Association's Indiana Fever and Megan Rapinoe of the National Women's Soccer League. As more players in the NFL and other leagues began to protest, controversy ensued.

One particular story caught our attention. The Kennesaw State college cheer team knelt during the anthem, motivated by and in support of Kaepernick. Shortly after we saw a local news story, Kim met some members of the team at a protest march and was struck by their determination and bravery.

Many of the athletes we mentioned suffered negative

consequences for speaking up: they were fined by their leagues, lost scholarships, were removed from their place on teams, or even had their careers cut short. As we reflected on the history of athletes and activism, we realized athletes who speak up for what they believe have long paid a price— especially those who are among the first to take a stand.

Today, the photo of John Carlos and Tommie Smith raising the Black power fist at the 1968 Olympics is an iconic symbol of protest. However, at the time, they, too, paid a price for their activism. They were stripped of their medals, sent home by the United States Olympic Committee in disgrace, and struggled to maintain a career in their sport for many years. Australian athlete Peter Norman, who stood on the podium with Carlos and Smith and supported their action, was ostracized in his home country. His record-breaking performance was overlooked, he was not selected to compete in the 1972 Olympics, and decades later, he was not welcomed to the 2000 Summer Olympics in Sydney.

With all of these significant moments in sports and cultural history swirling in our heads, we decided to tell the story of two friends on a high school cheerleading team who choose to kneel during the anthem. We wanted to explore the impact such an action might have on the characters' lives and their friendship.

We had completed an early draft of this novel and were

deep in the editing process during the summer of 2020 when a powerful wave of demands for social justice swept through the country. That summer changed many things, including the official stance of the NFL on athletes who kneel during the national anthem. National sentiment seemed to be shifting toward a more supportive posture. We were faced with a dilemma: Do we incorporate that changing sentiment into *Why We Fly*?

Standing up for what you believe is always a brave choice—particularly when many in the public square would prefer you to "shut up and play." In order to honor the athlete-activists who, throughout history, have stood up even when their actions were not lauded, we decided to set the book during 2019. We wanted to examine and reflect on what it was like before that historic summer when the mood shifted, when leagues all over America paused to protest police brutality and injustice, when athletes' powerful voices rose together and impacted society. We hope our readers will continue to examine the effect activism has had on athletes' lives and careers before, during, and beyond the impactful summer of 2020.

And to John, Tommie, and Peter, Lee Evans, Larry James, and Ron Freeman, Colin and Megan, Eric Reid, Brandon Marshall, JT Brown, Gwen Berry, Maya Moore, Billie Jean King, Seth DeValve, Bruce Maxwell, Zach Banner and Julian Edelman, the New York Liberty, the

WNBA, and the Milwaukee Bucks, and countless other athletes at every level from professional to high school who've stood up for what they believe—we're inspired by your courage and your tenacity. This one's for you.

WHY WE FLY

KIMBERLY JONES
GILLY SEGAL

Why We Fly

sourcebooks
fire

Published by Sourcebooks Fire, an imprint of Sourcebooks
P.O. Box 4410, Naperville, Illinois 60567-4410
(630) 961-3900
sourcebooks.com

Library of Congress Cataloging-in-Publication data is on file with the publisher.

Printed and bound in the United States of America.
LSC 10 9 8 7 6 5 4 3 2 1

For my sister Audra, who has always been my biggest fan.
—K. J.

For Maryann, who is the rarest of friends.
—G. S.

WHY WE FLY

1

ELEANOR

I. Will. Fly. Again.

Every word is a squat, and every squat is a word. The mantra keeps me going, balancing on the stability ball as my physical therapist, Elliot, counts reps. That promise to myself holds my back straight and my hands steepled in front of me, even as my thighs burn and my knees shake.

I. Will. Fly. Again.

Every part of me hurts. I can't squat—not even one more time—and I think a headache might be starting. I want to stop. I need to stop. But Elliot is still counting.

"Eight more, Leni," he says. "Come on, you got this!"

I absolutely have not got this. He knows it. I can tell by the tight line of his mouth, the way he edges a step closer in case he needs to catch me before I fall. Elliot's been with me since the start, so he knows the signs. Though it happened all the time when I first began PT, it's been *months* since a bout of dizziness sent me off the ball. Elliot and I joke that I need one of those construction-site signs: 72 DAYS SINCE LAST WORKPLACE ACCIDENT. But who's counting? I mean, besides me. And Elliot. He probably charts every spill, slip, and stumble.

I am so not messing up my clean slate today.

Because.

Five.

I.

Four.

Will.

Three.

Fly.

Two.

Again.

One.

"Okay, that'll do it." Elliot's hand is in mine, helping me down from the stability ball. He holds on until he's sure I'm steady, but it takes me another few seconds to feel ready to let go. Hopefully, he doesn't notice. One thing Elliot doesn't know about me is how good I am at faking it, and it's best if we keep it that way.

"So, El." I sip water from my CamelBak bottle. It was super expensive—almost forty dollars at REI—but it's got a straw. I learned early on that throwing back my head after PT to guzzle water equals lightning-strike brain pain. "How close are we?"

How close am *I* is what I mean, but Elliot likes to tell me we're in this together. He said it during our intro PT session, after the first fall. He promised he wasn't giving up on me when I had to come back after the second fall, when the doctors started throwing around phrases like "prone to concussions" and "career-ending."

I wipe sweat from my neck with a towel, focusing on steady movements, wide eyes, good posture. I need to show him those markers that I'm stable, that I'm healing. We're four weeks out from the start of school.

Elliot taps on an iPad, entering whatever he records on my chart at the end of a session. "Looks promising, Leni."

That's all he ever gives me. *A little ways to go. Great day today. Solid improvement.*

I grit my teeth and then stop, because the grinding sends a bolt of pressure to my temple. I don't want to hear about progress. I need a *yes* or a *no*, and it can't be *no*. A *no* will kill me. I need to hear a *when*.

"Should I make an appointment with Dr. Ratliff? Might take me a few weeks to get in to see him. I could call, just in case. For when we're ready."

Elliot smiles at his screen and continues tapping, leaving me hanging. I stare at the side of his face, willing him to say, *Go ahead, Leni. Make an appointment with Dr.*

Ratliff so he can give you medical clearance to cheer senior year. *So you don't have to sit out your last year on the team, and your final memories as the Class of 2019 aren't limited to a physical therapist's office. So you don't miss your shot at cheering in college.*

Come on, Elliot. I try to beam my thoughts directly into his brain without ratcheting the pain level in mine up to a twelve on a scale of ten. *Say yes.*

He sets the iPad on his desk and turns to me. He's flat-mouthed for a second, but he can't hold it for long. Elliot has no poker face. Smiling so wide I can see his gums, he says, "Go ahead. Call Ratliff's office."

I punch the air. "YES!"

He points a stern finger at me. "Four weeks from now, understand? Not a minute sooner. You're not quite there yet. And try to remind yourself that medical clearance isn't going to wipe the slate clean. You may continue to have symptoms that will need managing."

His words deflate me like a balloon. I know it's his job to set "realistic expectations," but all I can focus on is getting that clearance. I'll deal with everything else later. "I got it."

I reach out to return the fist bump he offers, tell him I'll see him next week, and head outside, shoulders back, chin up, strides long and even. If only it were as easy to rehab my brain as it was to repair my fractured ankle. But I can't dwell on that. My ankle's completely healed. And

4

now I have official word from Elliot that my head is getting better too. That's enough for now.

Heat smacks my face like a two-by-four the second the automatic doors open. I squint against the summer sun, trying to remember where I parked. South lot? Or was that last week? I rub one temple, close my eyes, and try to picture Nelly's bright yellow car, which is on loan to me while she's at high-performance gymnastics/cheer camp. No mental image comes to mind. Dammit.

Maybe I just need a minute. I sink down on the bench outside the door, dropping my gym bag, slumping down to lean my head against the backrest. My ponytail makes an uncomfortable bump, so I pull the elastic out and let my hair poof around my face. I can practically feel it frizzing into a cloud as I sit there, but for once I don't have to worry. Elliot's PT practice is thirty minutes away from school. I'm not likely to see anyone I know around here.

My eyes drift closed again, and I try to empty my mind of any thoughts. That's as hard as anything else in therapy, even those stupid squats on the stability ball. Which someone should really rename the instability ball, given how much it quivers.

Stop! I order my brain. *No thinking.*

The trouble is, if I'm not thinking, all that's left to do is feel. The soreness in my thighs. The tightness in my ankle. The throbbing in my head. All the signs I usually try to ignore. The things that remind me how different my life is now. The pain that threatens everything I've worked toward for ten years.

I feel a thud on the bench beside me, catch a whiff of cologne that isn't quite strong enough to cover up the stench of sweat. I keep my eyes shut, trying to hold on to the moment of peace I'd *almost* reached. I need another minute for the headache to recede before I drive. Whoever it is will go away. They won't talk to me. No one would start a conversation with some half-dead-looking stranger splayed out on a bench outside a doctor's office.

"Greenberg, that you?" a deep, familiar voice says, closer to my ear than I want it to be.

Oh God. Please tell me that's not who I think it is. This office is so far away from where we live. I wasn't supposed to see anyone I recognize, let alone someone I *know*.

"What're you doing way up here? You see Dr. Ratliff too?"

I crack one eye open and peek at my benchmate.

Yeah, it's exactly who I thought it was. Sam Walters, a.k.a. Three. Franklin High's star QB.

Ah, damn. I need to sit up, cross my knees, gather my hair. No one sees me looking so busted—ever. I don't leave the house looking like this. I don't even come downstairs looking like this. A bolt of energy sizzles inside me…and then fizzles. I can't scramble to pull myself together. I hurt. And here's Three, inconveniently seeing me at my worst.

Ughhhhhhhh. I hate today.

Three's voice gentles. "Greenberg? You okay?" On the field, the offensive line can hear his baritone calling plays yards away. On campus, the stans can hear his laugh clear on the other side of the courtyard. But these words? This whisper? They're just for me.

"No." Double damn—I didn't mean to tell the truth. Why'd he have to sound so sincere?

There's a rustle, the crinkle of plastic wrap, and then something cool and soft touches my neck, bringing not immediate relief but the anticipation of it. I sigh and let the chill wash over me, soothing the fire in my skull. And I'm finally able to open my eyes without feeling like the sun is an ice pick stabbing directly into them. I swivel my head a quarter inch to look at Three. He sits to my right, hair in short, spiky twists, a day or two of prickly beard growth shading the light brown skin of his jawline. Looking ridiculously hot even dressed in loose gray sweats cuffed at the knee and a black tank top. His left arm stretches across the back of the bench, his hand disappearing beneath my hair, holding an instant cold pack to my neck with the perfect amount of soft pressure.

"Thanks," I say.

He nods. I slither up from my slouch, and for a minute, we're awkward—him trying to keep the ice pack on my neck, me trying to gather myself and whip the blond cloud around my head into a neat ponytail.

Last time I saw Three was at Roman's graduation party in May. I calculate in my head—a month and a half ago? That sounds right. We hang with the same people, go to the same parties, and sometimes sit at the same table at lunch. But that's as far as our relationship goes.

"I didn't know you were injured," I say as he relinquishes control of the ice pack to me.

"Hell no, I'm not."

I raise an eyebrow at him and tick off the evidence on my fingers. "You're outside an orthopedic surgeon's office, smelling like physical therapy sweat and Bengay, carrying instant cold packs in your gym bag."

"Can't pull the wool over your eyes, huh, Greenberg?" He rotates his right shoulder twice—his throwing arm. "Repetitive stress. But don't let Coach hear you talk about me being injured. If it got around, every squad we play would take advantage of my weakness. Could end my career."

I nod. Some people might be surprised to hear a high school kid talking about his career, but everything with Three is about that. He's so on the NFL track, it's not even funny. He'll probably make it too. Everyone says he's good enough. "Hence coming way outside the district for treatment?"

"Yeah. Funny running into you all the way up here."

Not really, considering Coach Pearce referred me to Dr.

Ratliff last year, after the first fall. "It's probably Franklin's secret clinic, where they send all the athletes who need to keep their injuries on the DL."

"Damn, you make it sound like an undercover doping ring."

I smile. "Everyone knows Coach Bill Brown would do anything to get his players to State."

Three flashes me a smile in return, quick as a four-minute mile and full of perfect teeth made cuter by the slender gap between the front two. "Anyway, how about you, Greenberg? You gonna be back on the sidelines this fall, cheering us on when we win that trophy?"

I feel the most nonsensical flutter in my stomach. *Absolutely not, Eleanor Greenberg*, I tell myself. Crushing on Three would be the world's worst decision. "Yes."

He glances from the ice pack on my neck to the doors of the ortho clinic behind us, his version of listing the incriminating evidence.

"Yes," I repeat firmly. I yank the ice pack off my neck and hold it out to him. It was a mistake to let him see how much pain I was in. "I'm fine."

He pushes it back toward me. "Don't be a hero."

"I'm not. I just have to get going." I drop the pack into my gym bag, but I don't rise. Triple damn. I'm not ready to drive yet.

"You waiting on a ride?" Three asks. He checks his

phone. "My brother won't be here for another thirty minutes, but—"

I hold up Nelly's VW-branded key chain. "No. I, uh, have a headache. I was waiting for it to go away before I got behind the wheel."

"Good," he says. "You can hang with me in the meantime." He leans over—arm brushing across the bare skin of my thigh and sending a shiver through me—extracts the ice pack from my bag, and puts it back into my hands. "And you can stop being a damn hero while you do."

My mouth curves up. "You drive a hard bargain."

"I do." He draws a line through the air from the soggy pack to my neck. "Ice it."

I listen. And then, to my surprise, he lifts his arm and sniffs his pit. "It's not that bad."

"What?"

"Before, you said I smelled. But it's not that bad. Not like after practice, anyway."

I shake my head. "Well, PT's probably not as demanding as Coach Brown's two-a-days. But you still smell."

"Harsh, Greenberg. Harsh. And I used some Axe too."

"Not sure which is worse." I wave my hand in front of my nose.

He laughs, and I can't help joining in. We don't usually talk all that much, but he's easy to talk to. And he clearly gets what it's like to be injured. He was right about the ice.

By now, the headache has died down enough that I feel ready to drive. I pull out the keys again and rattle them. "Hey, do you want a ride? Instead of waiting for your brother?"

He arches an eyebrow. "You sure?"

"You live in the same neighborhood as Nelly, right?" He nods. "It's not out of my way. And it's better than chilling on this bench for another half hour."

"Yeah. Okay. Let me just tell him I'm set."

He taps at his phone screen, then stands, and I lead us toward the south parking lot, crossing my fingers it's the right one, since I still can't recall where I parked. My memory's definitely gotten better over the last few weeks, but I can't pretend it's back to pre-fall condition. With only a month left before school and cheer season, this healing timeline needs to accelerate. Like, immediately, because wandering the parking lot row by row, trying to find Nelly's car, with Three in tow is one more humiliation I do *not* need. I find it a few rows in and breathe a sigh of relief. Three snickers when he catches sight of the bright yellow convertible Bug, Nelly's seventeenth birthday present from her dad, Mr. Irons.

"Can't believe she let you borrow this," Three says, slinging his gym bag into the trunk along with mine. "Isn't she completely uptight about her ride?"

"She is," I say as he tucks himself into the seat beside me. He's not built like a linebacker, but he is six foot three and broad shouldered. His twists brush the roof. "She'll kill me if anything happens to it, so hands in your lap for the whole ride."

"Yes, ma'am. Where is she this summer, anyway?"

"At a high-performance cheer camp where you get to train with former Olympic coaches."

"Yeah, she is."

If the camp didn't make a best-of-the-best list, Nelly wouldn't be interested. It's why she's so freaking good at everything she does. She makes sure of it. That's my favorite thing about her.

Despite my order to keep his hands in his lap, Three seems to be all over the car—taking up space, holding on to the *oh shit* bar, fooling around with the XM radio and singing along when he finds a song he likes. Being the superstar he is on the field and in the halls at school and at every party. Honestly, I thought that might be a front, that he couldn't possibly exude charisma *all* the time, but this car ride is proving me wrong. He's this ball of restless energy, which would normally irritate me. Like, just settle down for a minute, dude.

But in Three, somehow it's magnetic. My eyes keep sliding back and forth between him and the road, and I find myself wishing I wasn't driving so I could watch him bop along to the music.

No, I don't. What am I saying? I do *not*.

He directs me to a neat ranch house on a street a couple of blocks from Nelly's place. A rusty basketball hoop hangs above the garage, and a football tackle dummy sits abandoned in the worn-down yard. There are lines of dirt carved into the grass, and I know Three made those. I bet he's out here running drills 24–7. A floor-to-ceiling banner hangs in the front window, emblazoned with Three's number in Franklin's colors, blue and green.

"Which came first?" I ask, pointing at the banner. "The number or the nickname?"

"The nickname," he says. "My first coach—I was probably seven or something—used to say I ran so fast it was like I had three feet."

It's more sentimental than I would have thought. "Cute."

"When do you go back to PT?" he asks.

"Every week. Same time, same place."

"Me too." Suddenly, the phone I left in the cup holder is in his hands. He holds it in front of me so facial recognition unlocks the screen, and a few seconds later, his phone dings. Did he just text himself with my phone? "Maybe I can ride with you next week. In case my brother has to work."

He bounds out of the car, jogging into the house without a backward glance. With my number in his phone. I feel that annoying flutter in my stomach again.

2

CHANEL

When Coach Tarasenko calls for a volunteer, my hand shoots into the air faster than anyone else's. They don't even stand a chance. Because this is *my* chance to show a legendary cheer choreographer what I'm capable of. I was accepted to this high-performance cheer and gymnastics camp on the basis of an application and video footage of me and our team. They only accept twenty-five of the most dedicated and talented athletes per grade level nationwide, and the level of competition has been an adrenaline rush since the moment I arrived on campus. This morning's routine is difficult, but not for me. It doesn't matter that we've only seen it demonstrated once. I've done things like this before and done them well. I know I can do it.

Coach motions me to the front of the gym, which is way nicer than the gym at Franklin. The floor gleams, the UF gator mascot painted in the center polished especially bright. Championship banners hang from the rafters. Even the tumbling mats look brand new, without a nick or tear. This is the kind of place I belong.

I stand still, roll my neck once to the left, once to the right, and one last time to the left, loosen up my shoulders, and then let my arms hang easily by my sides. Now I'm ready to perform. I run through the routine in my mind so it seeps into my muscles. As soon as the music starts, I move. And when I do, it's like there is nothing in the room other than the mat and the music and me.

This routine is perfect for me. The performer has to have serious strength and demonstrate total control. All those days of weight training with the football team back home—lifting more than all but the linebackers, I might add—have paid off. When the music fades and I finish, hitting one last perfect mark, and the ambient noise in the room returns to me, people are applauding. Well, the instructors are, but that is what matters most. I smile at them as I wait for Tarasenko's verdict. He strides over to me, looking a bit clichéd in his eighties-movie-gym-teacher attire, complete with shorts, pale legs, and knee-high athletic socks. But he's nodding approvingly. *Yesssssss.*

"And who are you?" he asks, his Russian accent strong despite the flawless English.

Before I can respond, one of the junior instructors consults a roster and says, "Nelly Irons."

15

My jaw clenches. That nickname is reserved for people I can't tell not to use it, like my mother and my auntie. Unfortunately, when my auntie dropped me off at cheer camp, the instructors overheard her talking and decided that must be what I wanted to be called instead of my formal name, Chanel Rose, which is too exquisite a name to waste.

Too late. Tarasenko says, "Whoa, Nelly."

Yuck. Now I have to pretend this is the first time I've ever heard that pedestrian old joke. He's lucky he's such a well-respected coach.

"You did not disappoint me," he says. "You executed very well. What position do you perform?"

"I'm a base."

"Yes, that suits you. It plays to your strength and your size. We will spend this week working to perfect your stability and your power."

Sheesh, I wish they filmed these sessions, like my dad used to film every practice so we could watch it together. Athletics is a shared passion of ours. He played tennis competitively all though college, and his Atlanta Lawn Tennis Association A1 team has made it to the city finals the past four years. My mother spent her time taking my older sister, Alana, to Jack and Jill meetings, where they organized social events and philanthropic work for African American mothers and children. Alana loved going to Jack and Jill. She's even still seeing the boy, Sebastian, who was her escort to cotillion. My mom has never liked how often I miss meetings due to my cheer schedule, and she has never forgiven me for not attending my own debutante ball. But my father understood that performing with the team at State that year was far more important to me. I must admit, I also enjoy that it's a space where I'm able to thrive without being compared to Alana, as she never did cheer.

I square my shoulders and nod to Coach Tarasenko. "Yes, sir. I look forward to training with you and growing as an athlete by the end of camp."

I spin back toward the bleachers and notice the other girls glaring and rolling their eyes. I suspect they won't be rolling their eyes once *they* try the routine. I should have done them a favor and not gone first. Their attitude doesn't surprise me. I've long since given up hope of anyone behaving maturely in high school. I can't wait to finally start college next year. I was born for the kind of place where everyone is on my level and the experience matches my ambitions.

———

"It's going to be easy for me. My dad is friends with Steve Harris, so obviously I'm in."

The two girls in front of me in the dinner line are

talking so loudly. I didn't mean to listen to their conversation, but I'm now trying to conquer the whirlwind that happens in my mind when something piques my interest.

"*The* Steve Harris? The comedian who has like five game shows on air, plus the morning show my mom watches?"

"Yes. He's the creator of YVP."

Now I'm paying attention as I move down the buffet line. By the time we've reached the salad bar, which, thank God, lets me pile my plate with a rainbow of right choices, the girl is talking about an application site going live in two weeks.

"You should apply too," she says.

"You think your dad could hook me up?"

"I can't promise, but I can ask. Either way, with all your accomplishments, you're exactly what they look for."

"The scholarship would be amazing."

"It would," says the first girl, "but I'd do it just for the mentors they assign. Last year, my friend Melissa was paired with Dorothy Buckhanan Wilson, so you know she's in for sure when she pledges in college."

She's just mentioned my idol, the international president of the AKAs, my mom's sorority that I've been groomed to join since I could walk. I want to continue to ear hustle, but my body wants lean in and get more details whether they want me to or not. In the end, what do I care if they think I'm nosey?

"Hey, what's the name of the program you guys are talking about?"

With a definite side-eye, one of the girls answers, "The Young Visionaries Project."

That's all I need; her crappy tone and expression don't matter. I head off to my room to learn more. Fortunately, I'm not at home. My father would make some ridiculous comment about how I should exhaust my options with an encyclopedia set before I go to Google. As if the *Encyclopedia Britannica* would have information about the Young Visionaries Project.

By curfew, I've gone down a rabbit hole with no way out. YVP is a mentorship program that nurtures future leaders by pairing them with notable business executives and entrepreneurs leading up to and through their first semester of college. They're awarded some scholarship money and, more importantly, they get access to career counseling and networking opportunities with the mentors and other winners and alumni. I cannot believe this is the first I'm hearing of such a prestigious program, and I'm excited to share it with my guidance counselor, Ms. Murphy. I stay up late to study every kid selected in the last decade, the mentors, and the opportunities that are offered each year. Besides my idol, the website sparkles with pictures of past mentors from *Fortune*'s Future 50 companies, movie studios, and Silicon Valley tech entrepreneurs. The YVP winners have been interns on Capitol Hill and won college scholarships; one even went on to clerk for the Supreme Court. And five of them won an international business plan competition and got funding to create a start-up. This program could be a game changer. It's so freaking *me*! Best grades, community service, extracurricular activities, outgoing personality, and a winner's spirit. Me!

I open a Google Sheet and start listing the application requirements, comparing my current qualifications against those of past winners. I've spent my entire academic career accumulating accolades so I can get into the best business school in the country. I open a tab beside the one containing the Wharton School of Business early decision application I'm already working on and spend some time color coding all the things I plan to do in the coming year to give myself a competitive edge. I may have heard about the YVP mentorship only two hours ago, but I want it bad. I'm going to do the work required to see my picture on that website next year. I can't wait to tell Leni. This is a project she'll encourage me through.

3

ELEANOR

WYD later?

I laugh when the text pops up on my screen. He entered his name in my phone as Three. Just Three. No last name. No other identifier.

I feel vaguely giggly about his message, and that annoys the crap out of me. I am not a Three stan. There are plenty of those hanging around. No more needed. But I wonder why he's texting me. Why he cares what I'm doing. His message lights up my screen for a second time, and I glance around the living room, like I'm going to find the answer sitting beside me. It's three o'clock on a Saturday afternoon in the middle of July. Everyone I know is either traveling for the summer or working, two things I'm prohibited from doing. My plans are to finish the season of *The Real Housewives of Atlanta* I'm currently bingeing and then move on to *The Real Housewives of Beverly Hills.*

Three's probably out running drills in his front yard. There's no off season for Coach Brown's players. I'm sure he's just making conversation before asking me to drive him to PT next week.

> IDK nothing much

His reply comes quick.

> Lazy ass. Come work out with me.

I've been lounging on the couch, but when I see those words, I sit up so fast a pillow shoots off my lap and onto the coffee table, where it knocks over my LaCroix. I flail for the can, which is now spilling bubbles onto the rug, and drop my phone. As my hands work overtime to clean up the mess, my brain stutters to process the text. Work out with him? Why would he want me to do that?

I get an answer to my question quickly, even though I didn't technically ask it.

> I need someone to run with.

Okaaaay. Three wants me to go running with him.

Not exactly the same thing as asking me to hang out, but intriguing nonetheless. Three and I? We're not friends. Every time I see him, he's surrounded by other people—teammates, girls, his family. Three doesn't roll solo. He's the kind of guy who needs an entourage, already the star he'll be when he makes the NFL, I guess, but on a smaller scale. I should blow him off. I don't do entourages.

An inconvenient memory worms its way into my mind from last year—a crowded lunch table full of basketball players. A chair I had to share with another girl, onto which I could barely squeeze one butt cheek. Roman, starting varsity point guard, sitting four seats away, paying more attention to a popcorn-tossing contest than he was to me.

Okay, so I don't do entourages *anymore*. Besides, Nelly has a free night tonight, and we're going to FaceTime. I can't wait to see all the stunts she's learning at camp. And she's all hype about some program she found that she's dying to apply for. I smile. Of course she is. Trust Nelly to get accepted to the most prestigious gymnastics/cheerleading camp in the nation and find the next thing before she's even completed the first.

I start to type the word *no*, but my thumb hovers over the send button.

I'm curious about what a future Pro Bowler's workout routine is like. I wonder if I could keep up. I glance at the clock on my phone. I could go for an hour and be back before Nelly calls. When Three tells me he'll be at the Peachtree Park running oval in forty-five minutes, I text back a thumbs-up.

He's shirtless and sweaty when I arrive. But not sweaty like it's ninety-eight degrees outside and he's just walked a quarter mile from the parking lot. Not even sweaty like he's run a warm-up lap. No, Three is dripping like a wrestler trying to make weight.

I stride to where he sits on the grass, knees bent, arms slung loosely around them. My hands settle on my hips. "You already started?"

"Nope." Three squints up at me, raising a hand to shade his eyes. Even his arm is sweaty. "Just got here."

"Then why are you so—oh my God. Did you *run* here?" He grins. "It must be six miles from your house!"

"Don't have a car," he says.

"I would have picked you up."

He gets to his feet and uses the shirt he's been sitting on to blot his forehead. "It was a good warm-up."

Oh. Six miles was his warm-up? My stomach ties itself into a little knot. This workout might be more than I bargained for. But I refuse to let him see that. Instead, I bury Nelly's keys at the bottom of my gym bag, tightening my ponytail so it sits precisely at the crown of my head, and

24

start doing some stretches. He's already run. There's some exercise equipment by the playground, but not here at the oval. What exactly does he have in mind?

Three pulls a set of keys from his pocket and throws them in my bag, and while he's there, he helps himself to one of my water bottles. I side-eye him with my most intense look, and he gives me a cereal-box smile in return. My stomach swoops. Oooh, that's dangerous. *Eleanor, you are not here for the charm. You're here to satisfy your...curiosity about Three's workout habits.*

I let him keep the water bottle.

After I've stretched enough, I follow Three to the track. "Let's race," he says, shaking his arms and legs out and then crouching, ready to take off. He quickly straightens up again. "This okay for you?"

I raise my eyebrows.

"I mean your head. Is running okay?"

I tense up. I hate this question. Hate the doubt. Hate the worry. "It's fine."

"Cool. Twice around the track."

And that's it. He's off, two, three, four paces ahead already.

Usually, I wish people didn't know about my concussion. They're too solicitous, wanting to do everything for me. And they're too worried. Every mistake I make becomes about the injury, even when I promise them it's not. I see my parents exchange looks when I forget something, when I cringe or close my eyes or touch my head.

But Three asking if I'm okay and then taking my word for it? That was nice. Unexpected. I think of him offering me that cold pack and wonder if he knows what to do because he's been where I am. Elliott offered to introduce me to another patient recovering from a concussion. I said no. It doesn't really matter what it's like for other people, does it? It only matters what it's like for me. Maybe that was a mistake. This comfort I get from being around someone who doesn't need an explanation—I like it.

I catch up to Three, and we jog in tandem for a minute. But then he pulls ahead. That pushes my competitive nature into gear. I feel it like a jab in the back—like someone is literally spurring me forward. I push myself. A hair faster. A longer stride. *Go, Leni, go go go.* The mental pressure works.

Three's got his own need to win, of course. We trade the lead all the way around the oval. I keep watch from the corner of my eye. I can't look over at him because I don't want him to see the silly smile on my face. By the time we start our second lap, we've escalated to full-on running. I'm flying on the inside because I'm keeping up with him. It's work, and I'm sweating as hard as he is, but at least I'm not breathing like a freight train.

"You've got a good stride," he says. I can't believe he's

talking while he's running—we're really pushing now—but at least his words are labored. "Long."

I much prefer the frenetic pace of a routine, my brain working overtime, thinking three moves ahead, calculating where I am and where the rest of the team should be. It feels busy and challenging, and it revs me up. The solitude of running? The hours where the only thing to think about is the slap of your feet on the pavement? No. A blank mind is not peaceful for me. Or at least, it wasn't before the concussion.

"If Coach Greer saw you, she'd probably try to recruit you for track."

I shrug. She has, more than once. "If I didn't cheer, maybe."

"You could do both."

"Ha! Who has time for that?" But even as I say it, I remember he does. "Wait. You run spring track, right?"

"Just for conditioning," he says. "To keep me in shape for football."

His tone says it's no big deal, but that's the opposite of true. Buried in my memories from last spring is a faded image of Three at the varsity awards ceremony, which we call the Letterman Banquet, dressed in a button-down shirt and a red tie, striding across the stage like he owned it while all the other boys shuffled around, red-faced and awkward. I don't remember the awards he won or the records he broke, but I know there was more than one of each. I recall sitting at the banquet table, no awards to show after missing the entire season because of my injury, thinking, *Jeez, and I thought Nelly was an overachiever!*

I don't call him on it, though. The tightness in his voice, the way he got louder on the word *just*. It's not *just* anything, but he doesn't want to talk about it. Instead, I say, "I run so I can cheer."

We glance at each other at the same time. Catch each other looking. Smile matching smiles. I feel a bolt of heat inside that has nothing to do with running or the temperature.

For another hour, Three and I work out. He's a *machine*. He goes and goes, and keeping up with him becomes a serious problem. After a while, I can't pretend I'm not winded anymore. When the headache starts, I have to call it. I'm tempted, watching Three do one more sprint, to keep going. I always used to keep up at everything, even if it killed me. Nelly and I have a motto: *Second place is the first loser.* Watching Three sprint back toward me, muscles straining, arms pumping, strides eating up the asphalt of the track, a burst of adrenaline sets me trembling. Maybe I can—

No, I scold the competitive part of my brain. The part that never yields first. The sore-loser part that will ruminate on this for hours—days, even—tightening into a peach pit in my stomach every time I recall it, reminding me that I gave up. I have spent the last eight months learning how to talk louder than that voice in my head. *This isn't therapy. Elliot isn't here to catch you. You know your limits.*

I mean, I do *now*. Failing to know them *before* is the reason I'm not cheering.

Three races past me as I call time. He returns and holds out a hand for the phone we've been using to time the intervals, but I pocket it.

"Had enough?"

I pat the ground twice, tapping out. For a second, I'm not sure what Three will do. He's panting, but it doesn't seem like he's done. I bet he could keep going. Maybe he will. Maybe he'll say, "Nice workout, Greenberg," and jog away.

He doesn't. "Yeah, me too." He reaches into my gym bag and takes out my remaining water bottle, throwing back his head to take huge gulps. But he doesn't drain it. He passes it to me, still half full.

I roll my eyes. "Gracious of you to leave me some of my own water."

He grins and swings my gym bag onto his shoulder. I lead the way to Nelly's car, which I parked on the roof of the garage, because no one else ever parks there and Nelly would kill me if her door got dinged. I'm still surprised she loaned it to me the entire time she's away. I flinch when Three heads toward the stairs to the roof. My legs are almost sore enough to tremble. But I follow, because I definitely can't ask him to take the elevator. That would be humiliating.

When we reach the car, Three tosses our bags in the trunk and slides into the passenger seat without an invitation.

"Oh, I guess you think I'm driving you home," I say.

His humor fades, and when he turns to me, there's a hint of confusion on his face. Of course I'll drive him home. But I want to make him ask for it, just to see if he will. My poker face apparently needs some work, though, because it takes about half a second for Three to figure me out.

"I thought you'd never ask," he says. Not even like he's joking. Like I'm actually the one who asked.

I shake my head.

The driveway at Three's house is empty when we arrive, so I pull into the center of it. He doesn't get out of the car. "Coming in?" He looks at me, all extra-dark eyes and charming smile and strong shoulders. I should say no. Why would I go into his house?

"I owe you a bottle of water."

I mean, he kind of does. He drank at least half of mine. But my house is only a few minutes away. I could get water there. I *should* get water there. I've already enjoyed hanging out with him too much.

I pop the trunk for him to get his bag, and then… I cut the engine.

I'll only go in for a minute. Just to get a drink. I leave my phone in the car to prove it.

Three's house is a shrine to football. The front room has been converted into an exercise room with a treadmill, an elliptical machine, and balance balls. It's actually a pretty decent gym. The machines look new, and there's a huge collection of free weights. It's better than any of the hotel gyms we've used when we travel for competitions. Three banners hang on the wall—UGA, University of Miami, and LSU.

"Which one's the favorite?" I ask, gesturing at the banners. Three's been getting looks from college programs since he was a sophomore. It's not exactly a secret—Coach Brown makes sure everyone knows when his players are getting the attention he feels they deserve. And Three's dad makes sure people know when Three isn't getting the attention he feels is deserved. Mr. Walters tweets so much game film of Three that he practically owns high school football Twitter's favorite hashtag: #fridaynightlightsga.

Three points at the UGA banner, then Miami, then LSU. "My dad, oldest brother, second-oldest brother. The brother right above me went to UGA, like my dad, for a little while. But he burned out. Coach Brown was pissed about that. Messed up the perfect family record."

I search my memory for information about Three's siblings but come up blank. "You're the youngest of four boys?"

"The surprise baby. Ray is seven years older than me."

Ah, phew. I don't remember because I never knew, not because it's information the concussion stole from me. They graduated long before Three and I started high school. "You going to uphold the family tradition at one of these places?"

"I'm not going anywhere that has a double-digit rank." Confidence radiates out of him. Like he's one hundred percent sure he's going to the best football school in the nation, in the universe. The way he says it, the way his shoulders straighten and his jaw flexes, it's impossible not to believe him.

"It's too soon for you to decide where you're going," a deep voice rumbles from the doorway. Blocking the way to the kitchen, I see Three as he will probably look in thirty years. His skin is darker than Three's, he's four or five inches taller, and a paunch puffs out the midsection of his crisp maroon polo shirt. Their jaws match perfectly, though, as do their wide-set, sparkling eyes. "National Signing Day isn't until February, is it, Samuel?"

The cockiness seeps out of Three like air from a balloon, dragging his shoulders down an inch or two, pulling the smile from his face.

"Yes, sir," he says. "I wasn't being serious. Just talking."

I imagine Three's been picturing Signing Day, when he'll sign with the football program of his choice, since he was a little kid. It has gotten to be huge deal for the top prospects. It's even broadcast on one of the EPSN channels. Three strikes me as the kind of guy who has practiced in the mirror how he's going to settle a college logo hat on his head and just the right proud-but-humble smile to go with it. I guess I can't fault him. If we make it to Nationals this year, I suspect I'm going to be practicing my TV smile too.

"Better not be, son," Mr. Walters says. He steps into the room and eyes Three, who's nodding to the floor. Then his gaze shifts to me. He looks so much like Three that it's a little disconcerting, especially because I've never seen that level of intensity on Three's face before, except on the football field. I feel like his dad is trying to melt my skull so he can see directly into my head. He holds out a hand. "Lamont Walters."

He envelops the hand I offer with a bone-breaking grip, the kind that would make a reasonable person flinch. I don't. A strong handshake matters, my dad has always said. He drilled that into me and my brothers and made us practice with him and each other until he felt our firm handshakes were above reproach. I used to curse him for it as I iced my sore hand when Seth and Daniel took it too far and left bruises. I'm grateful now. I squeeze Mr. Walters's hand hard in response and am gratified to see one of his eyebrows quirk up.

"Leni Greenberg," I say. And then, as if he cares, I add, "Three and I go to school together."

"Is that so?"

"We were just running in the park," Three says.

"Hmm. Let's keep our minds on the plan. We've been executing flawlessly so far, and we all know our strategy will get you to the top-ranked school on National Signing Day. But it does not involve any information leaking before we're ready, is that clear? It does not involve you running your mouth to impress a young lady."

Wow. It's kind of amazing to hear how invested his dad is. I wonder what it would be like if my parents had a whole strategy related to my competitions, like Three's do. Or even if they just sent me to all the camps Nelly's parents do.

"No, sir. I'm all in, I swear. Leni understands. She does cheer on the competition squad."

My cheeks warm, even though the AC is keeping it perfectly cool in the house. I like how he said that. He didn't call me a cheerleader, with all the connotations that normally accompany the word. The ones his father is obviously thinking anyway as his eyes snap back to me. I shrink down, hating myself for it even as I do. His scrutiny and the fact that I don't yet have medical clearance make me wonder if I get to claim it. Can you call yourself a cheerleader if you can't compete?

Mr. Walters leaves any comments he might be tempted to make in his own head, where they belong, and turns his attention to his son. "You have your third shake today?"

"Just got home, I was going to make it—"

"Three, how many times have I told you? You cannot skip them. You have to bulk up before the season starts, and you are not going to do that by running three-a-days in this heat and not drinking those shakes."

"I wasn't skipping, sir, I was—"

The front door opens, and another voice interrupts. "Whose car is blocking my garage and leaving me parking out on the street? That better not be one of Three's little friends."

I jump and swing around. Three's mom stands in the doorway, a cardboard box brimming with food in her arms, a huge pink purse dangling from her elbow. I've never been introduced to them, but I recognize both of the Walters. They're fixtures at games—Mrs. Walters up in the stands, Mr. Walters stalking along the fence, yelling to Three. She looks as agitated now as she does when we're down by more than two touchdowns and Three's throwing dead balls.

"I'm sorry, that's my car. Or my friend's car, but I'm driving it. I didn't mean to block you."

Mrs. Walters's eyes lock on me. "And who are you?"

Her look is not a welcoming one. It's as intense as Mr. Walters's, but where his was analytical, hers is critical.

"Leni," I say, struggling to hold back a flurry of blinks.

"Help your mother with the groceries, Samuel," Mr. Walters says.

Three is already on his way toward her. He gently extracts the box from her hands. "She's a friend, Mom." He kisses her cheek and takes the box into the kitchen while she removes her shoes—a pair of beaded platform sandals I've been coveting at Macy's for a couple of weeks—and rests them on a shoe rack beside the door. I go hot, wondering if I should have removed mine as well, regretting that I've tromped all over their clean beige carpet in grassy tennis shoes. Mrs. Walters, meanwhile, looks like she stepped out of a fashion influencer's feed, styled perfectly from those sandals to her silky tank top to her sparkly earrings.

"I'll move my car."

"Uh-huh, you do that," she says, following her husband into the kitchen.

Three catches up with me in the driveway. Parked at the curb is a dark red Suburban with the lift gate up. The trunk is packed full of boxes like the one Mrs. Walters carried in and Costco-sized packages of paper towels and toilet paper.

"Your parents are a little…" I trail off, jangling my keys and carefully considering how I want to describe them. I have a sense that he's pretty close to them, and I don't want to offend him. "Strict."

"They're not that intense all the time. You'll get used to them."

I *will*? I do my best to hide the shiver those words send down my spine and pause by Nelly's car. "I should—"

"Help me with these groceries?" He knocks his shoulder into mine. "Least you could do after kicking my mom out of her own parking space."

"Hey!" I follow him down the driveway so I don't have to yell for the entire neighborhood to hear. "You could've told me not to park there."

Three thrusts two humongous tubs of protein powder into my arms and piles a box on top of them. I groan under the weight.

"You got the guns for this, Greenberg?" he taunts, and I immediately stop staggering and heft the box.

"Please," I say. I'm straining, but he does not need to know that. "Of course I do. Let's see what you've got."

And just like that, it's a competition. We're egging each other on, tucking paper towels under our arms and using our chins to balance a cantaloupe on top of a stack of boxes. It only takes two trips to unload the entire car, and I feel a little let down when we've settled the last of the supplies onto the kitchen counter. Which is embarrassing and ridiculous, because who wants to keep unloading groceries? Ugh, I am glad Three is not a mind reader.

His mother intercepts us as we're walking back toward the front door.

"You're going to put away those groceries now, right, Samuel?" It's clear from the way she says it that this is not a question. It's also clear that company is not required for this part of the task. I've been dismissed.

"Yes, ma'am," he says automatically. "Be right there."

He walks me to the car and leans to open the door for me. Even as I'm rolling my eyes, because it's kind of a slick move, my stomach is swooping; no one has ever done that for me before. We freeze for a moment, Three looking at me with those smiley eyes. He sways closer, and for a wild second, I think he's going to kiss me. But then he glances at the house, where his mother stands on the porch, staring at us unabashedly.

Three watches me back out, which for some reason makes me an even more nervous driver than Nelly's constant questions about how her car's doing. My foot's never been as gentle on the gas as it is when I reverse out of his driveway and head home.

4

CHANEL

Mom is supposed to be waiting in the airport cell phone lot when my flight arrives. Ten minutes late, she texts.

> Just pulling up. Where are you?

I roll my eyes. I literally just told her. She's probably talking on her phone and not paying attention. And yep, she is. I see as soon as her silver Lexus SUV screeches up to the curb that she's holding her phone in her left hand, trying to pretend like she's not talking on it so the airport cops don't ticket her. I wonder if she lost another Bluetooth headset or if she just didn't bother to put it on.

She throws a slight wave and a big smile in my direction and pops the trunk so I can load my bags, but she continues her conversation as I slide into the front seat beside her. I shut the door, and she pulls back into traffic. I can only hear her side of the call, but I can tell she's talking to her assistant, Rita, about the children's hospital charity ball. She must be getting good news, because her voice is all high pitched, like it always is when she gets her way. She's wanted her company, Pearls and Petals Premier Events, to be the preferred partner for this fundraiser forever. It sounds like it's finally happening.

"Really? Front page? Well, second page? Okay, I can live with that, as long as it's a full page." She looks over at me and flashes another grin, this time accompanied by a thumbs-up. When she hangs up, she squeals. "Baby, you will not believe what just happened!"

"Oh yeah? Tell me."

"They're going to display the Pearls and Petals logo— we're an official sponsor of the ball this year!"

Official sponsor, not a hired vendor. That's pretty cool. "What did you have to give to get that?"

"A significant discount on my fee. But it was never about that, anyway. You know how important this event is for the medical community, and I'm happy to be involved."

Hmph. It may be important in the medical community, but it's also a good look for her and Dad and his work. Probably half the guests will be clients on his sales roster. I bet his company made double their normal sponsorship donation this year, and that's what that full-page ad for Pearls and Petals is really about.

"That's awesome, Mom. Congratulations. Count me in to volunteer and help in any way you need." This is a huge event, and the extra volunteer hours will look good on my applications. I need to remember to add it to the list I'm keeping in Google Drive.

"That would be amazing. I'll reach out to Alana as well. I have no doubt she'll come down and be involved."

Even out of sight, Alana is never out of my mom's mind.

"Oh, and I forgot to mention! I'm also heading up the planning committee for the Letterman Banquet in the spring."

"That's exciting. They're so lucky to get you. Now that event can finally live up to its potential."

"My sentiments exactly," she says.

Mom has to go see a florist for a wedding she's planning, so she drops me off at home, air-kissing me out the door. It's a bit surprising that she's taking meetings this afternoon, since we haven't seen each other in a month. I was looking forward to telling her all about my triumphs at camp. You'd think that after all the money she and Dad spent on this experience, she'd be eager to hear about it. But I get that her business is too small to have much staff, and she can't let her clients down. So I head straight to the laundry room, because I cannot even bring my bags into my bedroom without washing the camp funk off of everything. As soon as the first load is in the washer, I call Bunny, a nickname only I use for Leni. But she doesn't answer. I hope nothing's wrong. Actually, I hope she's not stalling because my car's not in the same pristine condition I left it in. So I text her that she better get her butt over here with my car.

You're home?

Is she for real? She had better not be cleaning up some Coke spill in my car.

Yes. I've only been texting you for three days, telling you what time my flight landed.

There's a pause, and I see the three dots appear and then disappear and then appear again.

I just forgot.

That's weird. I thought her forgetfulness was getting better.

How's PT going?

It's fine.

Okay. Just checking. Anyway, is the Bumblebee really okay? You better not have scratched up my paint job.

The Bumblebee is fine, I swear.

So you on your way here or what? Missed u, can't wait to hug my Bunny.

Lol. I know you mean hug the Bumblebee.

I laugh. She knows me too well.

Both of you.

It shouldn't take Leni long to get here, but it will probably be about a half an hour. On time for her is fifteen minutes late. I'm used to it by now, especially since I figured out the trick—you just have to tell her to meet you twenty minutes before you actually want her to show up. But now I'm stuck waiting. I put a few things away in my room, which, thankfully, is exactly the same as I left it when I went to camp. If Alana were still living here, she would not have managed to keep herself out of my stuff. The house is so much more orderly since she left for college. Summers are quieter, though, without her asking me ten questions an hour about what I'm doing and not even waiting for my answers before telling me ten things she needs me to know about her day.

Maybe the house is *too* quiet. I need a distraction while I wait for Bunny. But first, I need to put away my special makeup bag, which I wedge into its home behind the old radiator.

After it's hidden, I head out to the porch and take a seat on the swing. From the looks of it, my parents have spent the entire time I was away in the front garden. Mom's the gardener, but Dad knows how happy a manicured yard makes her, so he spends about as much time out there as she does, even though it's hell on his knees these days and his doctor would prefer he didn't do it since he also refuses to give up tennis. It is the nicest yard in the entire neighborhood, with manicured shrubs that never look overgrown and flower beds that are updated seasonally, so it's worth it.

While I wait for my perfect little Bumblebee to turn onto the street, I pull up *The South Cheers*, which is this blog that posts updates about everything that's going on in the cheer community from Virginia to Florida and Georgia to the Mississippi. It can be a good source of news, and it supposedly highlights sportsmanship, but sometimes it's just shy of a messy cheer version of the *Daily Mail*. The woman who runs it is a former cheer mom; her kid aged out a long time ago. Despite allegedly not having a bias toward her daughter's former team, it's obvious she still has favorites. There are certain teams and people she highlights more than others. She hardly mentions Franklin, for example, though we almost made it to Nationals last year.

I managed to keep myself from looking at the site while I was at camp through sheer willpower and because I know there isn't much real news in the summer months. But now that the cheer season is about to start, useful information will go up. Maybe some of the schools that start earlier have made captain announcements, and I can trust *The South Cheers* to be on top of that.

And yes, there is it—the south Georgia schools are up already. I scroll through the blog, which prints not only names but also pictures with the announcements. I see a few faces I recognize from State last year. I also spot a reference to the same high-performance camp I just attended in the blurb beside one girl's photo. I remember seeing her face, though we didn't really engage. I'm annoyed that her summer seems to be moving faster than mine. She's already got her C. I wonder how Coach Pearce is making the decision for our team. I've earned that C, and I look forward to seeing my photo on this blog in a few weeks.

I hear an engine coming up the otherwise-quiet street and check the clock on my phone. Yep—thirty-five minutes to the second from when Leni texted. She pulls my car slowly into the driveway, into my spot on the left side, and I run down the steps even before she's out the door. I spread my arms wide and race toward her, but just as she opens hers to grab me in a hug, I dodge and lay myself across the hood of the car instead.

"Bumblebee!" I croon, patting the perfect yellow paint job.

Leni laughs, shaking her head. "Well, hey to you too."

I throw one arm around her shoulder, squeezing her tight. "I missed you, Bunny."

"Go ahead. I know you want to do it. Bumblebee is ready for your full inspection." She waves a hand over the car like she's a game-show model displaying a prize.

"If you insist." And I really do it too. I was serious that she had better not damage my car, but she knew that. I can tell she took good care of it. There are no scratches, no dings, not even a stray piece of pine straw on the floor mats. The only weird thing I notice when I turn the car on to test the engine is that my preset radio stations have been changed to rap.

I shut the car off and fold my arms. "What did you do to my settings? When did you become a fan of Migos?"

"What?" Her face looks genuinely confused, so I'm guessing this is not a prank.

"Leni, are you okay? Did your doctor say something?"

Bunny gets kind of pink, like she does when she's keeping a secret. "I already told you, I'm doing fine."

"Okay, you obviously have some things to tell me. Come inside—I've got a six-pack of lemon-lime LaCroix, and it seems like we're going to need all of it."

She bounces after me to the house, making me laugh and reminding me how she got her nickname. She doesn't actually hop around anymore like she did when we were in Miss Boston's Tumbling Tots group when we were four, but she still walks with that little spring in her step that makes her my Bunny.

I take her out back, and we sit among Mom's herbs, which have almost overtaken the deck. It's nice because it always makes the air out here smell like mint and makes me think of Southern sweet tea. Leni fidgets with a trowel Mom must have left out while I crack open the LaCroix cans and set them in the koozies we had printed up for the squad last year, the ones that say FLY HIGH, DO OR DIE in green-and-blue script. She is still not ready to talk, so I examine her for a minute and notice some serious definition in her shoulders. She's tan, too, which is a surprise for someone who supposedly spent the last three weeks resting and bingeing Netflix. I thought I was going to be the one with the captain-ready body, but Leni looks even better than she did before the first time she fell.

"Your shoulders look amazing," I say. "Is that from physical therapy? I need that workout plan."

She goes completely red in the face.

I thump my seltzer can down on the table and turn to her. "What is going on with you?"

"It's not, uh, physical therapy. I mean, not completely."

Leni does not stutter. Now I have to know what she's keeping from me. "Just spill it."

"I've been working out a little extra this summer."

"What? The doctor said you couldn't work out alone yet. Bunny, you should have waited for me to get home. I told you we'd have time to get you in shape before the season started. You shouldn't have taken the risk."

"I wasn't exactly working out alone."

"With who, your brothers? I thought they weren't coming home from college this summer."

"Actually, um, it was Three."

I feel my face crumple up in surprise and maybe a little disgust. "Like, football Three?"

Leni glances at me and looks away again immediately. "Yeah. We ran into each other one day."

"Where did you run into him?" I snarl.

"At the park," she says. "I don't know, we ended up working out together, and then I gave him a ride home."

Now I get it. "Is that how my radio got turned into trap village?"

She grins at the table. "Yeah."

"Well, I know you didn't get those shoulders from one workout. Did you guys hang out again or something?"

"We've kind of been hanging out every day for the last few weeks."

I realize my muscles have not relaxed since this conversation started. "Why?"

"I don't know, Nelly." She twists the koozie around and around the can. "We've been working out. Don't make a big deal about it."

"Do we need to have a life choices discussion right now, young lady?" I reach out and take the can from her, forcing her to look at me. "You went down this road with Roman. I thought we agreed we were not going to get distracted. This is our year to make Nationals."

She looks at me, her big blue eyes a little watery, and I feel bad, because maybe I was shouting. Leni wasn't a crier before the concussions, but she's more sensitive now, and sometimes I forget to look for the signs.

"I'm not distracted, I promise. Look, it was good for me, right? You noticed the shoulders."

I can't argue with that, so I just sniff.

"It's a good thing. He pushes me."

"As hard as I do?"

"Even harder, if you can imagine that."

"Impossible. Maybe I'll have to come see for myself next time you guys work out."

She laughs, and her tears recede, so I slide the LaCroix back across the table to her. He pushes her? *Oh, Bunny.*

49

Why are we doing this again? It's no different from when Roman started paying attention to her last year. When Three ghosts her, like Roman did, I'm going to have to reroute her back to our goals. This is not part of the plan. We have to focus on making Nationals.

"Anyway," I say, "on to more important things. I've learned how we can take our pyramid to the next level but with some better safety precautions in place. Pull up your calendar. We need to start scheduling practices."

5

ELEANOR

In the week leading up to The Appointment with Dr. Ratliff, I ignore my 5:30 a.m. alarm twice. I turn it off without even hitting snooze. One morning, I sleep an extra four hours. My routine since freshman year has been to wake up early, eat, work out, grab a snack, and start my day. No days off. Since Nelly came home, she and I have been working on the bones of an epic new pyramid that will rack up points on the competition score sheet, plus I've had PT sessions with Elliott. I guess some additional tiredness is to be expected, but I haven't been this exhausted in a while. After the first concussion, an early alarm never bothered me, and the headaches went away within a few weeks.

That one was the *mild* concussion, Dr. Ratliff likes reminding me.

I don't like remembering the second fall, the not-mild

one, but the moment runs through my mind like a GIF. It was December and too cold and rainy to be outdoors, so we were practicing in the gym, sharing the north end with the JV squad while wrestling warmed up on the other side. The accident happened on an advanced dismount from our very wobbly pyramid. Still, it should have been a simple basket catch with Nelly and Avery Monaghan as bases and James Prince as back spotter. We'd done a similar stunt hundreds of times. I don't know what it was about that day. The gym was humid, and I was sweaty, though practice had only just begun. The JV girls were rowdy, and the wrestling team was loud. But I was fine. I was focused.

Until I wasn't.

I've dissected that careless mistake in my mind a million times, and I still can't pinpoint exactly what went wrong. Whether I looked down or to the side or threw my body weight just enough to get out of position. Whatever caused it, my shoulders shifted. My head was too far back. James tried to compensate. I heard him yell, "Shit!" as I came down wrong. He was a good spotter, and I'm sure he'd been tracking me closely. He and the bases tried to grab me, but I flailed, trying to save myself too. My head thwacked James's shoulder on the way down, then hit the mat. One leg bent under me, and my ankle collapsed. I didn't realize at first that I'd fractured it, partly because I blacked out briefly, and when I came to, the throbbing in my head blinded me to all the other pain. Nelly told me later that they didn't know if I'd cried out, because they couldn't hear me over the screaming of the JV girls and the wrestling coach yelling for someone to call 911. She also told me she insisted on riding in the ambulance with me rather than Coach Pearce and that my parents both showed up at the hospital within five minutes of our arrival.

I don't remember anything else from that afternoon.

After that fall, my early-morning alarm felt like a jackhammer in my eye, even when I lowered the volume so much I could barely hear it. We bought blackout curtains for my room because I couldn't open my eyes with any amount of sunlight streaming in the window. The longer the concussion effects wore on without improvement, the more stressed I got, and the more stressed I got, the less the effects improved. When the team went to State without me, the insomnia began. I lay awake for hours and then couldn't get out of bed because my body was just. so. tired. I was irritable all the time.

I started using an alarm again in June, and now I'm fine with it as long as the volume isn't too high. I haven't had a morning where I ignored it completely in months. I know it's the stress. Too much is riding on this appointment. Everything is.

When I finally get out of bed on the day of The Appointment, I head toward the kitchen. I don't do anything without fuel. Besides, it doesn't take much brain-power to whip up my staple, the egg white, arugula, sprout, and chèvre omelet I've made every morning since Nelly and I discovered Quinoa Mitchell's *Healthy Mornings* cookbook when we were twelve. I'm not as hard-core about it as Nelly, who makes a different recipe from the Quinoa plan every day.

Day 0. You ready for it?

Three's text puts a smile on my face. We haven't spent much time together since Nelly came home, but he gets it. With his season opener just a few weeks away, Coach Brown has the team doing two-a-days, and Three's dad has him on a bulking-up regimen I couldn't hope to contend with. I'm a little surprised—and kind of thrilled—that he remembered my appointment date. I reply with the 100 emoji and take the stairs two at a time, feeling just fine.

Today, I put the wheels of my life back on the track. Monday, school starts. Nelly and I will put our plan to make Nationals into high gear. We'll do athletic résumés and send them to college coaches. All the things we wanted before my concussion are within reach. I'm ready to fly again.

I just need Dr. Ratliff to say so on that medical clearance form.

I pause in the entrance to the kitchen. My mother and father ping-pong around, doing their chaotic getting-ready-for-work dance, passing each other coffee mugs, checking the weather app, packing lunches. I haven't seen it much this summer, since I've been off my routine. I smile, bizarrely relieved that this will again be the background to my mornings once things get completely back to normal.

They go quiet when they see me enter, their eyes running over the cheer warm-ups I dressed in for good luck.

"Morning," I say, heading to the refrigerator and trying to dispel the ominous feeling that accompanies their silence. I glance over my shoulder and catch them mouthing things at each other. They stop when they notice me looking.

"Big day today, huh, Eleanor?" my father says.

"Well," I say, "today's the day when one man has the power to put me back on track or end my cheerleading career entirely. So I guess you could say it's a pretty big day."

Mom sighs. "Leni, you're working on keeping your expectations reasonable, right? Dr. Ratliff warned you that some of the effects of severe concussions don't ever go away. I'm worried that if you don't hear what you want to hear today, it's going to…derail you."

The words fly across the room and smack me in the face. "You think he's not going to clear me?"

"It's a possibility. He said—"

"Did he call to give you a heads-up or something? If you know, you have to tell me."

Dad puts a hand on my shoulder. "Take it easy, Leni. We don't know anything. No one called us. We're trying to be supportive."

"We want you to know that no matter what happens today, you have other options, if you're willing to explore them," Mom adds, and I flinch. She sings this song on repeat, and I've never liked it any better than I did the first time. "You always have."

If they'd been trying to support me, they would have driven me to PT for the past eight months. I bet they've been half hoping this concussion would put an end to cheerleading. I know they blame my grades on all the time I spend at practice. They can't be honest with themselves about the fact that I'm not an intellectual like Seth or a math prodigy like Daniel. They don't want to accept that cheer is my only real shot at differentiating myself on college applications, despite the fact that Franklin's guidance counselor said that very thing to their faces.

My nose wrinkles as I fight back a sob. I am not going to cry over this. "I don't want those options. I want to cheer."

They exchange another Meaningful Look, the one they always throw around when they're tired of trying to get through to me.

My phone dings with another text from Three.

> Hey, so how about I give you a ride
> this time?

"Your appointment is at eleven? I have meetings on campus until ten thirty." Dad pulls out his phone and begins thumbing through screens, no doubt checking the busy schedule he keeps as the director of the university Hillel. "Maybe I can move a few and give you a ride there."

Nelly also offered to drive me. But if there's a chance to spend some time with Three, I'm going to take it. "I've got a ride. I'll see you guys after."

One of them sighs, but I can't tell who. I've already spun back to the fridge.

————————

A huge navy-blue pickup, the kind with the extended cab, pulls up to my house at exactly ten twenty-five. When I reach for the door handle, the door flies open, and a linebacker-size guy who looks a whole lot like Three steps out. One of the brothers, I'm guessing. Three is driving. He slings one arm over the passenger seat beside him while his brother pops open the rear door of the cab and slides in.

"Get in, Greenberg. Day Zero, right? Can't be late for that."

I look pointedly at the squished seat in the back, where Three's brother has angled himself sideways to have enough space for his legs. "I can sit in back."

The brother waves me off. "Three yammered at me the whole way over here to let you sit up front," he says. His teasing smile lets me know it's Three he's annoyed with, not me.

"Shut up, bruh," Three says, sounding not very menacing at all.

I'm going to make us late if I stall any longer, so I settle in beside Three, who pulls away from the curb. He leaves his arm across the back of my seat. I hate that I notice that, but I do.

"I didn't know you had your license," I say.

"Of course I do. I just don't have a car," he says.

"Yeah, 'cause then how would Dad the drill sergeant keep tabs on you at practice, make sure you're running the full hundred," his brother mutters. I glance over my shoulder and see that he's looking out the window like he's not part of the conversation, except he must be listening pretty closely.

"Ray." Three's tone is flat and serious.

"It's the truth. A car is equal to freedom in his mind."

"Man, you know it's not like that. Dad's just keeping me focused on my plan."

"Your plan? You the one who decided to set the alarm

for a six-mile run at four a.m.? You the one who dictates drinking three protein shakes a day? You the one tweeting game film at scouts? You the one taking out loans to pay a personal trainer and maxing out credit cards on a professional-grade home gym?"

Three begins twirling one of his twists between his fingers, and it's clear he doesn't like the way this conversation is going. It's also clear Ray can't stop. It's way too hot in this car, and I surreptitiously fan myself with the collar of my shirt. We roll to a stop at a red light, and Three drums on the steering wheel, banging out an irregular rhythm that's nowhere near in time with the music on the radio.

"So he's wrong for wanting to give me the best shot at making it? We both know those are all things I need to get me where I want be."

"And if you never earn those league paychecks? Then what?"

"Just because you didn't make it doesn't mean I won't," Three says quietly. But not quietly enough.

Ray scoffs. "I *did* make it. I have the life I want. You all act like the choices I made are some kind of failure, but you're delusional if you think the only valuable things in life are the ones Dad and Coach Brown tell you to want."

Dear God, I have never wished so hard for a magic wand in my life. The only thing I want to do right now is whisk myself a trillion miles away. I'd rather be having the worst PT session of my life than overhearing this family spat. We don't do this in my house. When anyone in my family gets mad, they get quiet and excuse themselves from the conversation. The tension level rises skyscraper high for a week, and then we get over it, but we don't talk about it, and we certainly don't fight about family matters in front of strangers.

Luckily, we're pulling into the clinic parking lot. This torture will be over any minute. I just need to hold out until we arrive, and then I can flee.

Three navigates to the front of the building, and I'm out the door almost before he stomps on the brakes. I'm maybe a foot away from the car when I hear Ray shouting. I glance back and see that he's switched into the driver's seat and rolled down the passenger window. "Hey, Three. You invite shorty to the Labor Day cookout? Bet you didn't, 'cuz you know that's not part of *the plan*."

Oh. My knees lock. A cookout. That I am not invited to. I'm not going to look at Three. I will melt into a puddle of humiliation if I do. I can't help myself. I glance over. A scowl snarls his features. He shakes his head at his brother, but then he catches sight of me, and his body droops.

"Leni, just ignore Ray, okay? He's full of it, like always. Come on, let's get this medical clearance that's coming your way."

He takes my hand and doesn't let go until we're ushered

into Dr. Ratliff's office, which is a small industrial room with a fake wood desk and bookshelves laden with medical textbooks, two chairs, a few degrees on the wall, and nothing else. The room smells of disinfectant and cologne.

Three lounges in one of the uncomfortable chairs, tall enough that his feet reach all the way to the desk in front of him. I pace.

"How many?"

"What?" I pause by the window, which overlooks the parking lot. I wonder if Dr. Ratliff is too low in the hierarchy to merit an office with a view. Maybe that means we shouldn't take his prognoses too seriously. We should probably get a second opinion. Why didn't we ever think to do that?

"Steps," Three says, halting my mental horses before they bolt. "Between the door and the window. I know you're counting."

A faint smile creeps over my lips. "Twenty-three, and how did you know?"

"It's what I'd be doing if I was you."

God, how does he always just *get it*?

"It's okay you're nervous."

The words of protest die before they exit my mouth. I never tell people this stuff. It's not what they want to hear. But in this too-warm room that smells of bleach, I suddenly feel like I can say what I want to this boy with the

Crest-toothpaste smile and a guaranteed future in a professional sports league. "I'm scared as hell."

I flop into the empty chair beside him and lean back.

"What if he says I'm not cleared? What if he says I can never cheer again? Every time I get a headache or forget anything, I get nervous, and then I worry about getting nervous, and then I get a headache. I'm running on this hamster wheel, and I'm constantly afraid that before I have a chance to step off, I'm going to get flung off and fly smack into a wall!" I crook an elbow over my eyes. "Just so you know, if he says I'm done, I'm probably going to cry."

Three slides his hand between the chair and my neck, cupping it, his skin warm and soft. He squeezes gently. "I can handle it."

"I can't." We're quiet for a minute, and I'm grateful he doesn't spout a bunch of BS about thinking positively. Or worse, repeat all the crap my parents get into about having "other options." His silence wraps me in a cocoon and asks nothing of me, and it's peaceful in my mind for a change. "What would you do if someone said you couldn't play anymore?"

He expels a loud breath. "You go right for heart, don't you? I can't even think about it. I've got nothing without football. It's all I do. It's all I am."

I lift my arm and peek at him, eyes burning. His face is grave. This is why Three always gets it. "Same."

"So," he says, his voice dropping to husky whisper, "how are we going to celebrate when he clears you?"

I raise an eyebrow. "By getting back to practice, finally."

"Where's the fun in that?"

"You're one to talk. You work out like it's your job."

"It is my job. But I know the difference between a job and a celebration. Come on, I'll take you for ice cream."

I laugh. "That's it? That's your idea of a big celebration?"

"My dad always took me for ice cream when I won a game in peewee. Just the two of us. My mom would go back to the house with my brothers, and we'd go to Carvel, and he'd get me two scoops in a waffle cone. *With* sprinkles."

Oh dear God. Why is that such a cute story? If I were a Southern belle, I'd be having the vapors. But, I remind myself, I am not a Southern belle. And ice cream is not in my diet. "We always went to Dave & Buster's. I'm the reigning Skee-Ball champion of my family. I like to celebrate a win with another win."

"Hard-core, Greenberg." He slides closer, close enough that our knees touch. "How about we go after this? You can win me one of those ugly stuffed animals from the claw machine."

"For real?" Is this… Is he asking me on a date?

He leans closer, and I freeze, dying for him to kiss me and feeling ridiculous that I'm so desperate for him to kiss me that I'm willing for it to happen in this doctor's office.

"Yeah, for real." Three's hand slips from the back of my neck over my shoulder, fingers trailing along my skin. My breath catches, and he stops, his mouth hovering close enough that I can smell a hint of the blackberry-and-mint gum I know he keeps in his pocket. His deep brown eyes watch me intently, but he waits. Waits for me to decide what I want. It's not as difficult a choice as it should be. I lift my face, and his lips brush mine gently at first, and then he presses closer, and we fall over a cliff into the kiss.

The door flies open, and Three straightens up. I jump back and pull my hands away from him, folding them in my lap. Dr. Ratliff walks in, his white coat flapping around his thighs.

"Sam," he says, the sound of a barely suppressed smirk in his voice. "Nice to see you, though it's a bit of a surprise, considering this is Eleanor's appointment."

"Had to make sure my number-one fan was ready to be on the sidelines, cheering me on while I throw those touchdowns, Doc."

I swing an elbow into Three's unprotected side. He laughs and rubs his ribs. Dr. Ratliff takes a seat behind his desk, squirting a blob of hand sanitizer into his palm. I stare at the repetitive motion as he rubs it in, and my amusement fades. I feel my cheek muscles sink and drag the grin off my face, replacing it with the hangdog look I wear when I'm worried.

"Okay, Eleanor. I'm sure you want to get right to it," the doctor says, booting up his computer. "After a second impact like you had, it's important to ensure that you're completely symptom-free."

"I am, Dr. Ratliff. I promise. I'm ready to go back to cheerleading."

"You know you're three to five times more likely to suffer additional concussions now, right? You're at heightened risk for long-term cognitive impairment."

My hands tremble. The first time I heard those words, I didn't even know what they meant. I do now, and there isn't much that scares me more than permanent brain damage. Except having to give up the only thing I've ever really been good at.

He looks at me hard. "And your goal is still RTP?" I nod. Yes, all I want is to return to play. "Okay, then. Let me compare your recent post-injury results to your baseline."

The doctor clicks around interminably on the computer, reading with his mouth pursed. I clench my fists and think *please, please, please*. Besides me, I hear Three's breathing speed up.

"Well, Eleanor, I have to tell you…"

Please, please, please.

"Your scores have returned to baseline, and your exertion test results were normal."

"Yeah!" Three leaps out of his chair and punches the air.

I'm not ready to celebrate yet. "Does that mean I'm cleared?"

"Based on this post-impact assessment, I'll clear you to return to play under the following protocol." Dr. Ratliff types as he talks. "One week of noncontact drills. As long as your symptoms do not return during that time, then—"

"I can fly again?"

The doctor smiles. "Yes. You can fly again."

I'm crying. I thought I'd cry if he said no, but here I am, tears trailing around my nose and dripping into my mouth. I try to wipe them away, but Three grabs me and hugs me tight, pressing my face into his shirt. Oh, gross, I'm snotting all over him! He doesn't seem to mind, though; he just runs his hand over my hair again and again, letting me sob.

Dr. Ratliff prints out the note I so desperately need and hands it over. "All right, you two. Get out of here and go celebrate."

Three sets his hand on the small of my back and propels me from the office. "Yes, sir, this girl's got a game of Skee-Ball to win."

Three decides we need a whole group to celebrate with. While he texts his teammate and best friend, Bull, to come get us, I can't stop staring at the clearance note. I text a picture of it to Nelly, who replies with about fifty confetti emojis. I can barely see them through the tears, which won't stop falling.

"You're back," he says, tapping the page. "Has it sunk in yet?"

I shake my head. I wonder how long it'll take.

Three throws an arm around my shoulder, smiling. "Listen, you should come to our house on Labor Day. For the cookout."

A thrill runs through me, but the echo of Ray's words in my mind brings it to a halt. "You don't have to say that."

"The guys from the team will be there. You could bring your girl, Chanel."

He twirls the end of my ponytail softly. From the corner of my eye, I see an older lady with carefully curled white hair emerging from the passenger seat of a sedan in the valet line. Her mouth quirks into a knowing smile at the sight of us. I imagine her speaking in my grandma Joan's voice. *Enjoy that one, dear*, she would have said in her sassiest accent. *He's a cutie.*

He is. But an hour ago, this cutie didn't want to acknowledge that he wasn't inviting me to a party he's now telling me to come to. I don't want him to do it because Ray shamed him into it. But he said the team would be there. Maybe this whole thing is no big deal to him. Maybe I'm overthinking. I should stop doing that. Nelly's head might pop off if I suggest we go, but she'll do it if I really want to. Probably.

"Maybe," I say to Three, thinking that if Nelly goes, I will.

6

CHANEL

"Hello, Ms. Robertson," I say to my favorite school secretary, who's at her post at the front desk and buzzes me into the building. I've been looking forward to chatting with her. I know she's going to want to hear all about the people I met and the things I experienced at camp. You can always tell she's actually paying attention, and she remembers every detail you share with her. It is odd to see her without her usual ill-fitting cardigan. The staff isn't required to dress up right now, since school isn't yet in session. Her Falcons T-shirt stretches too tight over her chest, and the collar sits too high on her neck. I see that her hair, which has always teetered on the edge of bad eighties prom, has not improved since I saw her last spring.

"I see the team spirit is back in the building," she says as I set my bag on one of the chairs in the reception area, settle down next to it, and cross my ankles. "Tell me about your exciting summer. I know you must have done something grand."

"I had the opportunity to train with Coach Tarasenko. He's the premier cheer coach on the Eastern Seaboard."

Ms. Robertson clasps her hands and leans over the desk. "That's fabulous. How long did you work with him?"

This is why I was looking forward to seeing her. She's one of my most attentive friends. "I was there for a month altogether. I originally intended to go for two weeks, but once I saw the caliber of the program, I convinced my parents to sign me up for a second session."

"I don't know what's in the water over there at your house, but whatever it is, your parents need to bottle it and sell it. You and your sister are two of the most amazing kids I've ever encountered at Franklin." She gestures at the shiny gold plaque hanging on the wall behind her. "What other student besides your sister has received the Governor's Academic Seal of Excellence? I don't have to tell you only one percent of the graduating seniors in the state receive that award. We're so proud, I don't think that plaque is ever coming off this wall."

As usual, Alana's looming presence outshines my moment. Sometimes I don't think I'll ever crawl out of the shadow of that plaque. I love seeing Ms. Robertson every day during the year, but it means I have to stand under that reminder of Alana's legacy. I have recurring conversations about Alana with nearly all my teachers. Don't get me wrong, I'm proud of her, but it's hard to measure my own success when it's constantly compared with hers.

A gentle *tap-tap* on the school doors draws our attention. Leni stands outside, bouncing on the balls of her feet, dressed in a pair of black compression shorts and a Franklin High Cheer T-shirt. Ms. Robertson lets her in and waves us toward the gym.

"Have fun at your first practice, girls!"

"Thanks, Ms. Robertson," Leni and I say in unison.

As we head down the hall, we dodge stacks of desks and chairs waiting for teachers to move them into classrooms for school on Monday and a janitor polishing the floor. From open doors comes a symphony of teachers chatting and papers being shuffled.

I'm bubbling with excitement to see the team's growth since the end of last year. "I can't wait to start this practice with those exercises I learned at camp. They will be a great test of everyone's summer conditioning."

"It's the first day back," Leni says. "People might need a warm-up before we go full throttle."

"Don't worry, Bunny. You're ready for this."

"Who said I wasn't?"

I slow my steps and let her walk ahead of me, stung. Bunny rarely snaps, and never at me. I remember from looking up concussions on WebMD right after her fall that moodiness can be a side effect. Hopefully it's just nerves. I've got bubbles; she's got butterflies. I decide to let her attitude slide. Right now, I need to focus on this practice and the elections that are being held at the end. A week ago, Coach sent us an email saying she'd decided to choose the captain through a hybrid process where the team votes and she has veto power.

I catch up to Leni at the gym door, letting it slam closed behind me.

"Hey," Chloe yells. She sits in the bleachers, talking with some other members of the team. "Welcome back!"

Of course it's Chloe. She's the sweet one. Beside her, Val slurps a twenty-ounce can of Monster Energy. My stomach turns just watching him.

"What?" he says, flipping his longish blond hair over one shoulder. "It was a late night—what can I say?"

"It's going to be an even longer day once you crash from that stuff," I say.

"And she's back," Gia says under her breath.

"Yeah, didn't realize Coach had arrived," Paris adds. "Oh, wait—she hasn't." Paris has been on my bad side ever since she started sucking up to my sister at Jack and Jill meetings. She appointed herself Alana's unofficial mentee. It's no surprise to me that she's already bringing the snark.

"Excuse me for trying to save that boy from a liquid heart attack on top of his toxic spray tan." I shake my head.

As usual, none of them can take constructive criticism. It's the reason we're all developing at different rates and haven't gelled as a team. I'm going to need to get them together, or Nationals isn't in view.

"Come on, y'all," Leni says. "All this fighting gives me a headache."

Sixteen faces turn toward her, some shocked, some sad, some wrinkled with worry. Leni grips the strap of her gym bag, drawing her arms in toward her chest. The last thing she needs is so many eyes on her.

"You know what, guys? My bad. We started off on the wrong foot. How about we do some stretches to relax?" I head to the center of the gym, patting Leni gently on the back as I pass. She lets out a small sigh, and her hands loosen.

One of my favorite things Coach Pearce introduced last year, when she started as our coach, was thirty minutes of yoga to start practice. She got the entire team on board and now it's almost everyone's favorite part of the day. We all grab mats, and I attempt to help Gia carry hers. She yanks it away and stalks to the opposite side of the circle. Clearly, someone is still upset, but now's not the time to engage with her about that. If we're going to get to Nationals, every minute counts, and we don't have time for Gia's petty nonsense. I sit down, and the team fills in the circle. Just as we've finished arranging ourselves, Coach Pearce arrives.

"Oh my God, you guys, what a great way to start this season!" she yells in her perky voice. She sounds younger than her age, which has to be midthirties, and it's the only thing I can fault her for. She has so much energy, and when we're struggling with moves, she is still capable of demonstrating them flawlessly. I looked her up online right after she was announced as the new coach and found photos of her cheering with her college team. Her ivory skin is still as youthful as it was then, and she's tall and slender with long hair pulled up in a ballerina bun. She usually dresses in well-fitted warm-ups. It's not a shock that she's already garnered admiration from our team, though it's only her first full season with us.

Her arrival warms the room. "Love this! You all came to play, day one. This is how a team takes Nationals."

The room fills with *woo-hoo*s and applause as Coach's wave of energy sweeps over us. Even Leni gets caught up in it, high-fiving Trin.

"To get the ball rolling, I want to hear one thing each of you worked on this summer and one thing you will do to help this team make it to Nationals next spring. Let's start!"

Skylar Lim goes first. "I watched videos of every winning routine in the last five years and took notes on all the stunts and pyramids. This will make it easier for us to plan a routine that tops all of the prior winners."

Huh, that's impressive. Skylar is one of our younger girls; she just made the competition team. I'm looking forward to seeing her analysis of those old routines and what she can do this year.

Avery goes next. He says, "I worked with a personal trainer on my upper body."

After the fifth person talks about their summer exercise regimen, I wonder if anyone besides Skylar and myself are going to have anything productive to add to this conversation. The one thing we're all clearly devoted to is the gym, but I think Coach is looking for more practical steps the team can take. That's why I'm excited when I look up and realize Leni is next.

But her head is down, and her eyes are trained on the floor. I nudge her knee to alert her that it's her turn. She peeks up, and there's a crackle in her voice as she says, "I'm going to keep the team motivated this year and focused on our goals."

That's what she came up with? We've had extensive conversations about our plans this summer. I don't understand how that's the only thing that came to her mind in response to this question. Is it possible she's not being honest with me about her health?

"Tell us about how you worked toward your recovery," Coach prompts.

"Oh. Uh, just with a physical therapist. The usual."

My poor Bunny. Of course that question about her health tripped her up. She doesn't need this group in her business like that. "Coach, I think Leni might be more comfortable talking to you about that privately after practice."

Leni's gaze drifts back to the floor, but not before she taps her sneaker against mine. That's our little way of saying thanks. We've been doing it since we were six.

To put a clear end to this awkward moment, I take my chance to share our plan. "Team, over the summer, I went to an elite stunt camp, and we worked on proper form and utilizing spotters. I know we can get more points for our routines with these techniques. Coach, if you don't mind, I'd like to demonstrate."

I position myself in the center of the mats. "Everybody up!"

Leni stands first. Nobody else moves, like they're a bunch of burnouts instead of an elite competition team. She says, "Wait till you see Nelly's routines, y'all. They're game changers. Perfect for an epic squad like us."

In response to her cheerful encouragement, they stand and join me. I grin. This is why Leni and I are friendship goals.

For the next ten minutes, I walk through Coach Tarasenko's tricks, and I'm thrilled to see the excitement on everyone's faces. When Chloe, who I usually stunt with, Val, our spotter, and I perfectly execute a two-man prep to a power press to a one-man liberty on the first try, the team actually applauds. Okay, now we're getting on track. This is how a winning team perfects its moves.

After that, we break into small groups, each with a base, a flyer, and a spotter, to practice. Within a few minutes, everyone is hitting their stunts. I watch with pride, counting *one, three, five, seven*. Yesssss. I did that.

"Chanel, you are our gemstone today," Coach Pearce says. She never names a star performer because she believes it's more important to reward hard work. So she names one gemstone every training session. It is a little cheesy, but a smile I can't suppress creeps over my face anyway. Not only do I like being the gemstone, I knew I would earn it.

"Today is the first day on our road to Nationals!" Coach says. "We're going take a quick water break, but before you walk off, come over to this table and cast your vote for the next Franklin cheer captain. Once everyone has voted, I'll tally the ballots in my office, and we'll reconvene for the announcement."

I stride over to the table and pick up a ballot before anyone else is off the mat. Leni is right behind me, Val on her heels.

After we're done voting, we head to refill our filtered water bottles. I feel energized. "I was concerned for a second, when everyone was acting more like sacks of laundry than athletes. But that ended up being a great first practice."

"The new Nelly techniques worked their magic."

"After you got them on their feet," I say. "Together, we are a force. Our skill videos are about to level up."

"I agree," Leni says, pulling up her phone calendar. "I'll make a schedule for capturing the footage, editing it, and sending it off to schools. Are University of Pennsylvania and Cornell still at the top of the list?"

We've been doing college research since freshman year, tracking the top business schools that also have quality cheerleading teams. It's finally time to set the last puzzle pieces of our applications into place. Cheerleading is the thing that sets us apart. Good grades and a few accolades aren't enough. Even the boost I'll get once they select me for YVP isn't enough. We need truly impressive résumés to stand out. For Leni, cheer might make the difference between acceptance and rejection, since her grades aren't the greatest. And a scholarship will justify to her parents why she should continue with cheer, even though they view it as a distraction from her studies.

As we gather back on the mats to hear the captain announcement, I try to stay calm. If you had asked me last year, I definitely would have thought Leni was my only competition and that we might be named cocaptains. But since her injury, she's been noticeably checked out. There are some others who have skills, like Chloe, but she can't be counted on to manage anyone but herself. Paris is also a strong presence on the team, but everyone knows she doesn't want the captaincy because she's too focused on other things, like Jack and Jill. So there's really just one possibility.

I keep my back straight, smoothing my shorts with my fingers, stretching my neck upward, standing directly in Coach's eyeline, making it easy for her to find me when she's ready. I take a deep breath and wait. Coach steps into the center of the circle, clipboard clutched to her chest. She rubs the whistle dangling from her neck.

"Let me start by saying this is not a decision I made lightly. There were a lot of factors to consider. Skill, commitment, leadership, and personality all played a part. The person who is capable of leading us to Nationals not only has to possess all these qualities but also must be someone I feel confident I can work with and count on. To be fair, many of you possess many of these qualities, which is something that makes me very proud to be the coach of this amazing team. In the end, there can only be one captain, and the team votes made it clear who you all trust and feel safe with. That was just as important as the other attributes I listed. I feel really good about this choice, and I'm thrilled to announce the new captain of the Franklin Rams: Eleanor Greenberg."

My eyes narrow, and I curl in on myself like a dodge-ball just pounded into my solar plexus. My body temp spikes. This makes no sense. Leni hasn't been a factor for a year. This position is about skill; it's not a popularity contest. How could Coach let this slide, knowing about her injury? How can my team not see that I've worked the hardest? They've betrayed me.

A small rumble grows into a roar of claps and cheers, and someone shouts, "Yay, Leni!"

Leni's back is to me, and she's surrounded by her new admiring subjects. I need to get out of here. I need to go find my sanity in the bathroom of the old locker room no one uses anymore since the renovation.

As I head out the door, I rifle through the pile of backpacks and snatch mine up, hopefully noticed by as few people as possible. My breathing has gotten heavy. Becoming captain was a major part of my plan. Now everything's off track. I can't think in this state. I need a moment alone to deal. I duck into my favorite stall, which has a window I can crack open. It won't open fully, but it's enough to get the ventilation I need. My towel sits on the window ledge, waiting for me. I pull it down and smooth it over the toilet tank. Then I hang my backpack on a hook on the back of door, pull out my flowered makeup bag, and hop up to sit on the top of the tank, checking to be sure nothing, not even my shoes, will be visible under the door. If I breathe quietly enough, someone could come in and not know I'm here.

I unzip my bag, squeeze my knees together, and take out the pieces of my vape pen. I check to make sure it's fully charged, connect the base, load the cartridge of Runtz, press and release the button, and take a short breath. I exhale a stream of vapor just as the door swings open.

I'm so caught off guard by the squeak of the hinges that I cough and the noise echoes around the room. There goes the silent operation that I've perfected over the years. I wave my hand around, trying to dissipate the vapor. My mind is in such a frantic state that I leap to my feet to continue slapping the air, and everything on my lap goes crashing to the floor. Being caught is my personal apocalypse. Whatever hope I had of covering this up comes to a cinematic end as my pen rolls under the stall and bumps into a spectacular custom-painted sneaker. A hand with chipped blood-orange nail polish and way too many plastic promotional bracelets picks it up, then taps on the stall door.

"You dropped something."

I clench my jaw for a second. "You can just leave it in the sink."

Dear God. I pray this person doesn't know what the vape pen is. I hear it clink into the sink, the squeal of the door opening, and a soft slam. I let out a sigh and clean up. I wish I could teleport into tomorrow. I slip my arms through the straps of my bag, filled with AP textbooks, and shuffle it around until it's evenly balanced on my back.

I look around the stall, checking that I collected everything, and notice my towel. I can't leave that here—it's not safe anymore. This was my spot. What would even lead someone else to hang out here? I stare at the towel, wondering how long ago they discovered my place and whether they use my towel too. I look around for a plastic shopping bag, though I know I probably won't find one, but I need somewhere to stash the smelly scrap of terry cloth. It's saturated with the scent of my secret, which isn't such a secret anymore. Of course, there's no bag. With no other options, I toss the towel out the window. It could have been left outside by anyone. It could have nothing to do with this bathroom or me.

I shake my hands, letting my eyes rest on the graffiti I've studied every time I've sat in this stall, taking a minute to calm myself. One puff would have been enough, had my unexpected guest not blown my high. I run one finger over the initials and words carved into the wall. It might be the last time I see these.

What am I going to do now that this place is compromised? I can't sneak off campus or go out to my car. It's not like I do this all that much—just when I need to manage a little stress. I wouldn't have needed it today, and wouldn't have jeopardized my spot, if that freaking captaincy hadn't gotten away from me. My mind goes blank, like a GPS does when it can't connect with a satellite. I'm just spinning and spinning, and I have no idea which way to go. But I know I can't stay in here any longer.

I push the stall door open, and there, leaning against the sink closest to the door, is Marisol Fuentes. I don't know her well, but we've been in classes together. She's the only student who scored higher than me on the AP Calc exam, which I guess is not a surprise for a girl who aspires to be the future administrator of NASA, which we all know because she makes an annual Career Day presentation about it. She also heads the Gay-Straight Alliance. Marisol's arms are crossed over a sleek black blazer. Underneath, she wears a gray graphic tee with hot pink lettering that reads *Woke Up Lesbian Again.*

"You're going to need more than that open window to get rid of the scent of that loud," she says with a smile that's almost a smirk.

I clap a hand to my chest. That was a bullet I did not expect and can't dodge. "I don't know what you're talking about."

Marisol makes the universal gesture, pinching her thumb and forefinger together and bringing them to her mouth. "I'm talking about marijuana. Reefer. Kush. Mary Jane. Dope. Pot. Weed. Wacky Tabacy."

Is this girl ever going to shut up? My eyes feel like they might pop out of their sockets.

"Doobies. Blunts. Cannabis. Hashish. Grass. Any of

this ringing a bell, considering you were just smoking it and that's your vape pen in the sink?" She picks it up and twirls it between her fingers. "It's a nice one. Clearly you're a connoisseur."

I wish Scotty would beam me up. I wish I were wearing ruby slippers I could click together. "That's not mine. It's not what you think it is."

Marisol laughs and shakes back her bangs. "Dude, the gig's up. What's the big deal, anyway?"

"The big deal is that smoking in a bathroom is for burnouts, not future Harvard MBA students."

"And yet, here we are."

"Are you going to tell?" I ask.

"Tell who?"

"I don't know, everyone on Snapchat?" I glance at the door. I need to get out of here. If Marisol showed up, someone else could.

"Now, what would I gain from doing that?" She crosses one foot over the other, leaning back against the sink again, casual as a character in a movie.

"The satisfaction of being the one who saw me when I was low."

"Outing people just ain't my bag, Chanel," she says. "Your secret is safe with me."

I consider her for a moment, searching her face for the lie. I don't see one. "Thanks for that."

"I've been low before too. And tried this." She taps the vape pen against the sink. "As a way to distract myself."

Part of me wants to dig deeper, but that's not the nature of our relationship. "I'm sorry to hear that."

She studies me for a moment, then nods. "Why are you feeling low?"

"I don't know." You know what? That's bullshit. I do know. "I was just robbed of being elected cheer captain. I worked hard for it. I trained all summer. When everyone else was messing around, I was practicing. But apparently, hard work was not a prerequisite. They picked Leni instead."

Even Leni has to know she's not in top form. She's been out for almost a year. How is it possible the team thought someone who's been sidelined for that long was a better pick than me?

"You're right," Marisol says. "That's jacked up."

I feel a little warm glow that someone understands.

"You're certainly bossy enough."

The warmth becomes a burn. Marisol is just like everyone else. "Well-behaved women rarely make history."

"Oh, shit. You're right. I guess I need to check my internalized misogyny. Don't ever let anyone tell you how to behave."

"Trust me. I don't."

She dangles the pen before me. "Then go stick up for yourself."

I can't explain why, but her words motivate me. It's time I spoke with Coach Pearce.

By the time I get back, the gym has cleared out. I head down a hallway toward the coaches' offices. Through the window in the door labeled CHEER, I see Leni sitting on the couch with an unfocused gaze, while Coach talks spiritedly. Only a few minutes pass before they finish and Leni emerges from the office.

She smiles. "Thanks for waiting. Let me just grab my bag, and I'll be ready to go."

I can't believe she jumped straight to that. "I need to talk to Coach first."

It's clear when the revelation hits her—her whole face crumples up. Does she not think I deserve a conversation? Even if she was the Leni of last year, before her two accidents, I would still deserve some insight into why I wasn't chosen. She's just going to have to wait.

"If that's what you feel you need."

That comment doesn't warrant a response, so I turn and slip past her into the office.

"Chanel!" Coach says with a too-bright smile. She keeps her office cozy with a couch and throws instead of a desk. She directs me toward the seat beside her, crosses her legs, and rests her hands on her knees. "I thought I might be hearing from you tonight."

Of course, I think, *because you already know how unfair*

this choice is. I sit with my back so straight no judge could take a deduction due to form. "I admit I'm surprised by this decision, Coach. I thought my summer training, my routine accuracy, and my leadership abilities would have made me the obvious choice."

Her lips pull back in a strained attempt to maintain her smile. She shifts, crossing her legs the other way. "You're a star, no question about that." She laughs uncomfortably. "But there's a difference between an individual star and a team leader. Based on the votes, it was clear to me that the team feels safer under her leadership."

Safer? That's dramatic. If anything, my focus on accuracy keeps them safe. I have no idea what this woman is talking about. I am constantly offering advice and working to enhance the skill of my teammates. Everyone else acts like an individual. I'm the only one who tries to guide the others.

"Coach, I realize this is only your second year here. Perhaps you haven't had enough time to assess. But one thing is for certain—I have been an integral part of build-ing this team."

Her face tenses. The put-on smile she's been wearing drops. "I know, and that's why I'm counting on you to support your friend and be an influencer in the locker room."

An influencer? What am I, some D-list social media

celebrity? This dismissive response is not worth my time. I stand and smooth my puff back into place. "Well, thank you for your time. I know what I need to do now."

"I hope so, Chanel."

I shut the door gently behind me, because my mother taught me never to show your hand when you're plotting. Slamming a door would definitely reveal my hand. As I leave Coach's office, I feel a vibration in my bag and reach for my phone to see a text from Leni, saying she's gotten a ride with Three. Ugh—I thought she would be past that summer fling by now. School is starting. It's time to get focused. I'm low-key glad she left, though. I can't be bothered with her right now.

When I arrive at the Bumblebee, I tune SiriusXM to the baroque station, close my eyes, and breathe. The Young Visionaries Project application waits for me at home, and that is the most valuable use of my energy going forward. Leni can take care of the team and begin to appreciate what she's gotten herself into.

7

ELEANOR

August barrels toward September, leaving me without a minute to rest. My days are filled with practices, reviewing routines with Coach Pearce, watching video to see what the team's strengths and weaknesses are, and all the preparation those things require. I thought Nelly and I would be doing this together. She has a better eye for technique than I do. If I ask, she looks at footage of something specific and tells me what's not working, but she doesn't volunteer her help. I understand that she's hurt, but I'm surprised by how far she's stepped back and how unhappy she seems with me. It's not like I campaigned to be captain. I didn't even vote for myself.

On top of my after-school commitments, class work has become my personal hell. I finish most assignments the period before they're due, working on them between classes, hastily submitting them via Google Classroom. At least half the work I turn in is late. When my grades start getting posted, my parents are going to be furious.

The only good news is that I'm flying and my concussion symptoms have not been affecting me too badly. Sometimes my temper goes wild like an off-leash dog in a crowded dog park, but not often. I think that's mostly stress, anyway.

I'm not complaining. This just...isn't how I expected senior year to go.

One evening a couple of weeks into the football season, I have a rare free moment to walk Hamilton, our only-slightly-out-of-control Bernedoodle, who's two but still acts like a puppy. Practice ended early because Val threw up. We didn't know if it was from exertion or if he was getting sick, and we couldn't risk the whole team going down with a stomach flu. So Pearce called it, and I'm home before dinner for the first time this year.

I don't know what to do with myself. The right answer is homework. I should work on my English essay or maybe prep for my Earth Science lab. And isn't there a precalc quiz on Monday? I should check the class website. But neither of my parents are home yet, and Ham is going crazy. He needs exercise. Maybe a walk around the neighborhood with him will help me focus on what I should do with the rest of this evening.

Ham and I don't run. He's not the kind of dog you can

jog with. The one time we tried, he chased every squirrel, rabbit, and falling leaf we passed and tangled the leash around my knees, then around a tree, and landed himself in a ditch. He's too curious for his own good. I stick to a brisk walk and try to keep him from wrestling trash cans.

After a block, Ham sniffs the air, loses control, and bolts. I haul after him, and we round the corner and bump into Ham's best friend, a fluffy little Pomeranian named Matzoh Ball, who's being walked by our neighbor three houses down. Our neighbor who is also our rabbi.

"Sorry, Rabbi Spinrad," I say as we do the inelegant untangle-the-leash dance.

"You know you can call me Ezra, right, Leni? We're not in synagogue."

I could, but it would be weird. I've known him well since he helped me through an uncomfortable situation a few years ago when Nelly and I joined a competition squad that prayed before every tournament—in Jesus's name. His guidance gave me the guts to ask the team to change the prayer to something more egalitarian, and he's been a close family friend since. But still—the man tutored me for my bat mitzvah. He wears robes to conduct services on High Holy Days, teaches Sunday School, and speaks in the gentle tone of someone who counsels for a living. I'd never call one of my teachers by their first name, and in the same way, I squirm at the thought of calling him by his.

"They make an odd couple, don't they?" Rabbi Spinrad says, gesturing at the dogs, who are jumping around and wrestling. Matzoh Ball bounces like…well, like a ball. Ham is an eighty-pound giant who could gobble him in one bite, but he's a gentle teddy bear. He's never so much as set his teeth on the little dog. "I think Matzoh Ball misses him."

Normally, the rabbi's wife brings Ham over to play in the backyard with Matzoh Ball during the day, but she got called out of town yesterday. "When's the other Rabbi Spinrad due back? Cutting it a little close to the big day, isn't she?"

"Babies don't take the High Holy Days into account when they decide they're ready to join the world. They're inconsiderate like that," he says with a laugh. "Dana's sister wants her to preside over the bris, so she'll be gone for a while. I'm afraid it'll just be me doing Rosh Hashanah services this year."

"Well, don't tell her I said so, but I've always liked your sermons better."

"You just say that because they're shorter."

I grin. "No way. She's better at chanting Torah, though."

"I'm rabbi enough to admit that," he says. "You used to be pretty good at chanting yourself. Any way I can entice you to make a guest appearance this year? We're still looking for a reader for the afternoon youth service."

I used to love doing that. At our synagogue, after your

bar or bat mitzvah, they let you come back and read Torah at services if you want to. I've done it a handful of times, and the youth services for families are my favorites. Those kids, a few years away from their own b'nei mitzvah who are starting to learn the prayers for their own service, look at you like you've won an Oscar when you chant a flawless haftarah portion.

My smile fades, and a guilty spiral swirls around in my stomach. "I'm sorry, Rabbi Spinrad. I don't think I can. I'll be at services in the morning, but we have an extra cheer practice that afternoon. I'm captain this year. I can't miss it if I—"

He holds up a hand. "No need to explain, Leni. Your team is an important commitment. I'm glad we'll get to celebrate the new year with you during morning service."

I know he means that, but it feels wrong telling the rabbi I'm working on one of the holiest days of the Jewish year. That it's more important to me. But honestly, it is. I'm sure my parents wish I wouldn't dip out of the luncheon we're hosting, but I can't ask the team to practice if I'm not there. That feels wrong too.

Wrong and right are supposed to be easy. I wonder when every decision started feeling like a shade of gray.

———————

"Girl, no," Nelly says, letting herself into my room. "That is not what you're wearing."

"What?" I look down at my shorts and yellow halter top, both of which are new. The shorts make my legs look tan. Nelly is wearing a royal-blue dress with cap sleeves and a V-neck and a hint of white lace along the hem. Okay, so maybe that's a bit dressier than I was expecting for a cookout.

Nelly's already in my closet, shucking hangers aside. "Where are your dresses? Did you hide them? Yikes, I can't find anything but yoga pants in here. We need to take you shopping."

I grin. My wardrobe never meets with her approval. Half the time when we go places, she doesn't bother with my closet and just dresses me from her own. She's her normal in-charge self today, and I love it. Away from school and the team, we're closer to the way we used to be.

Nelly emerges with a black-and-white color block dress with a slim waist and a flowy skirt that her mother bought me as a gift. She lays it on the bed with a very final sort of nod. "You'll present better in this."

"It's a barbecue, Nelly, not a job interview."

"That's what you think."

I don't know whether she agreed to go because I begged and she felt bad for me or because she thought she needed to keep an eye on me. Though I wore her down, she made it clear she is not into the idea of this party.

Once I'm dressed, I consider my shoe choices. Nelly

would pick the kitten-heel sandals, but I hate the way they pinch my toes. I rebel, going for a pair of black flip-flops. She clicks her tongue when she sees them but lets it go.

"Nelly, I'm really glad you're coming with me. Maybe after it's over, we can come back here and work on the pyramid a little? Maybe you could make a demo video we can post to the WhatsApp group?"

"I don't think I'll be able to." She opens my jewelry box and picks through it, which is her way of avoiding me.

"Come on, Nelly. I was counting on us doing this together. You've basically disappeared."

The lid of the box snaps shut, and she whirls around. "Captain is your responsibility, not mine."

"Yeah, but we both know I would have helped you if you'd won."

"I didn't, though."

Oh. That hits different. I knew she was disappointed, but Nelly wouldn't hold a grudge just for that. Her feelings are hurt. "Nelly—"

"We should go. You don't want to be late and make a bad impression on your little crush's family."

She clips out of my room, and I have to hurry to keep up.

———

Cars line the street near Three's house, and a stream of people heads toward the door, carrying dishes and trays of cupcakes. The next generation of athletic superstars—a horde of kids ten years younger than us—runs around in the front yard, throwing a football. An older man with graying hair sits on a folding chair on the porch, smoking a cigar and calling instructions to the boys that they mostly ignore.

The door stands wide open, and we follow the others inside. A TV blares from the living room, and laughter trickles from the kitchen. But most of the noise comes from the teeming backyard, where we find the bulk of the partygoers. There must be fifty people here, some crowded around Mr. Walters, who stands at a chrome grill, wearing an apron that says GRILL GOD and waving massive tongs. On the other side of the cement deck, another man has set up a tiny tailgate grill that gives off the powerful scent of charcoal. Mr. Walters's grill is certainly fancier, but the other smells more like a barbecue to me. The middle of the deck is taken up by two huge folding tables sagging under the weight of all the dishes people have brought.

Some nineties-sounding music blasts from a speaker attached to an iPhone. At the edge of the deck, people play cards, and all across the lawn, others sit around scattered tables, wearing sunglasses and laughing with one another. I scan the crowd, looking for familiar faces, and spot four or five members of the offensive line. Each of them has two plates spilling over with ribs, potato salad, coleslaw, and baked beans. A serving dish piled high with dinner rolls sits in the middle of the table.

With a little more than the usual spring in my step, Nelly and I head over to the two huge coolers beside Mr. Walters's grill. We squeeze the gallon jugs we've brought onto the edge of a table nearby.

"Hello there, girls," Mr. Walters says, waving us over. "Leni, isn't it?"

"Yes, it is. Hi, Mr. Walters. Thanks for having us."

He hums a response but doesn't say anything, and a flicker of discomfort flashes through me.

"This is my friend, Chanel Irons."

"Miss Irons." He nods. "What's that you brought to share?"

"Iced green tea with a dash of agave syrup," Nelly says.

"Agave." He nods. "I've been reading about that. It's a better option if you have to satisfy the sweet tooth. Very nice. Make sure you switch out a glass of that for that bottle of Southern sweet tea nonsense Samuel's been carrying around, thinking I don't see."

Nelly laughs. I feel a few of the soap bubbles careening around in my chest burst. I don't want to be jealous; it's silly. But I wish I'd gotten to give that answer and have Three's dad nod approvingly at me.

He looks past Nelly and me, shouting over our heads, "Ray! Bring that ice over here, son—the drinks are heating up. And where's your brother with the meat?"

"Right here, Dad," a familiar voice says. I turn and see Ray emerging from the house, carrying two bags of ice in each hand, and with him, Three, grasping a massive cooler, his forearms flexing. An adorable little kid with big beautiful curls and light skin trails just a step behind Three, carrying his own miniature cooler. He shares enough features with Mr. Walters, Ray, and Three for me to think he might be Ray's kid.

My stomach swoops all the way down into my shoes like I'm on a roller coaster. If the warmth spreading through me is any indication, my face has gone pink. I have got to get myself under control, or everyone is going to notice. But it's useless when Three catches sight of me and grins. I answer in kind, my smile stretching so wide my cheeks hurt. As he goes to set down the cooler, the sleeve of his Carolina Panthers jersey brushes the exposed skin of my shoulder.

"Hey, Greenberg," he says softly.

"Hi, Three," I whisper back.

We're not as discreet as we think. Nelly frowns at us, and Mr. Walters looks down his nose, his brow furrowed, as he notes how close Three stands to me. He's too attuned to it, and not in an indulgent way.

"You met my friends, Leni and Chanel?" Three nods at his dad.

Mr. Walters raises one eyebrow. "They introduced themselves."

The little boy grabs on to Three, who does a biceps curl, lifting the kid's feet off the ground, and they both laugh.

"Son, that's an eight-figure arm you're using as a jungle gym," Mr. Walters intones. "That arm just set a Georgia state record for most touchdown passes thrown in the game against McPherson last week."

Three beams and puffs his chest. But I notice he does set his nephew on the ground.

Ray swoops the boy up, glaring at his father. "Been a minute since I had to sit through a famous Lamont Walters Celebration of Meaningless Stats."

"Better a Lamont Walters Celebration of Stats than a trip down the Ray Walters Path to Working the IT Help Desk," Mr. Walters says.

Whoa. I glance at Nelly, and her face looks like my stomach feels—shriveled with discomfort. I've never heard any of our parents speak the way Mr. Walters does to his son.

Three takes my arm and begins shifting me away. "Sir, do you need anything else from me? If not, I'm going to show these ladies where to pick up their plates."

"Take Bryce with you," Ray says, handing over the little boy.

I feel the tension expand between father and son as they face off, but I let Three guide us away, resisting the urge to look back even as his nervous commentary distracts me.

"Come try the ribs—my dad is not messing around with the apron he wears. He knows how to cook 'em. Try one of my uncle's too—here, this plate. You can be the deciding vote in their running cook-off. Bryce, my dude, do you like PopPop's ribs better or Uncle Felix's?"

Bryce whispers, "Uncle Felix's, but don't tell PopPop I said that."

Our plates are soon loaded with the kind of food neither Nelly nor I ever eats, but we're too polite to turn it down. Three deposits his nephew at the kids' table and leads us to his friends' table. He pulls out chairs, shifting to make sure Nelly is on the far side of me. He's the last one to sit, squeezing into a too-tight spot between Bull and me. I'm not sure if it's an excuse to get close until I feel his fingers brush the skin of my knee underneath the table. I suck in a breath.

"Bull, how are those ribs? Who wins the cook-off?" Three says, pounding Bull on the shoulder as though absolutely nothing out of the ordinary is happening.

Maybe it's not for him, but I'm squirming. I scoop up a spoonful of baked beans I have no intention of putting in my mouth and then discard it in favor of a long drink of ice water, hoping to bring the temperature of my face down to a less noticeable level.

Three's hand stays on my knee for the rest of the meal.

8

CHANEL

So, this is what we're doing? Instead of something productive that's going to next-level us, Leni is over here trying to become a football wife like on those lowbrow reality shows she likes to watch. And I'm stuck speaking with the bro squad, which thinks a dissection of the Falcons' preseason stats qualifies as an intellectual conversation. Three is practically sitting in Leni's lap, and she apparently thinks the rest of us can't see it. I see all of his country preacher charm washing over her like a tsunami. It was all kicks and giggles with Roman, too, until he had to treat her with some actual respect, a task he couldn't manage.

This is supposed to be the year we dominate in all things. The two of us. We have a finite amount of time to walk across that stage victorious, in a way that tells the world we came, we saw, we conquered. What is becoming this boy's hanger-on going to do for her? For us? Nothing. The plan was already on its way to being demolished because of her unwarranted election to captain. And here she is, taking things even further in the wrong direction. I really need to spend time thinking about how I can salvage this year.

I might be stuck watching Leni audition to be Three's first-round draft pick for cuffin' season, but I can still find a way to stay on task. I pull up Google Drive on my phone and open my YVP essay questions, which I've been revising all week. A couple of my responses are not quite up to my standards—yet.

Out of the corner of my eye, I see Bull stand up, holding his chair to his behind, and waddle over to wedge himself in next to me. "You as bored as me watching them push up on each other all day?"

"It's a Planned Parenthood cautionary tale right before our eyes."

"Damn, okay, Nana Nelly. You went hard on that one."

"Just an observation." I turn back to my phone and type out a few more words.

"Whatcha working on?" he asks, leaning so close he bumps my shoulder.

I flip the screen facedown in my lap. This is not ready for other people's eyes at the moment. "I'm working on some essay questions for this opportunity I'm pursuing. It's called the Young Visionaries Project."

"Oh, I know about that. I was watching Steve Harris's

show with my mom one time when I stayed home from school, sick. He talked all about the applications he was reviewing. That's a dope program."

I should have expected this would not be news to Bull. He's the only football player I know who raises his hand in class and has the correct answers. I appreciated the debate we had last year in AP Brit Lit about creative use of language. Maybe he would have some good pointers on this essay. But before I show him the Google doc, we're interrupted by a gorgeously styled lady who approaches with a wine glass in her hand.

"Now, who do we have here?" It's Three's mom; I recognize her from the stands. She attends every single game wearing Three's number.

"Mom, you remember Leni and Chanel," Three responds, quickly scooting away from Leni. *Oh no, my brother, don't even attempt to use me as a pawn in the game you're playing for your mother. You already did that by telling Leni to invite me.*

"I'm Chanel," I say. "I came with Leni." I gesture in her direction so Mrs. Walters makes no mistake about who was actually invited. *Three, we are playing chess, not checkers.*

She smiles politely. "We're all moving inside now. Ladies, why don't you go join Three's teammates in the den? Son, you start cleaning things up out here. Help your brothers take these tables to the basement."

Leni stands up and starts collecting the trash. "We can help too."

Mrs. Walters sets three fingers on her wrist. "No, dear. The boys can handle it."

"Yes, ma'am," I say, picking up my own plate and heading inside. I cut my eyes at Leni. "We have to be leaving soon. But thank you for everything, Mrs. Walters. You did such an amazing job with this yard."

She coos. "Why, thank you. Chanel, was it? I see you have fine taste."

We dump our plates in the trash and slip inside. "Let's just grab our purses and go."

"Okay," Leni says. "I'm ready."

I think she gets that we're not really welcome here, but I'm sorry that she's sad about it. We head into the bedroom where they've been storing the purses and a few of the older guests' cardigans. It only takes a quick shuffle through the pile to find mine and then hers. I turn to hand it to her. Leni stands back a step, deep in her head, wearing her disappointment on her face.

"Oh, Bunny. Don't let everyone get to you. We never have to see them again."

She nods as we walk into the foyer. We've nearly made it to the front of the house when the knob of the basement door banging into the wall behind us makes us jump. I turn to see Ray. He throws his arms out and yells, "Leni, leaving so soon?"

"I guess so."

"No, you can't! You have to meet Aunt Rhonda. She's going to love you. I know you want to get out of here, but it'll only take a few minutes."

He puts his arm around her, almost swallowing her, and shuffles her toward the den. She turns back, giving me the Mayday look, so I follow.

In the den, the team sprawls all over the sofas, fighting over game controllers, the battle-style video game they're playing turned up to full volume. Mr. Walters enters at the same time as us, trailed by Three and Bill Brown, the football coach. Even though he's off work, there he is in a Franklin Rams polo shirt, like he's about to coach somebody from the den. His middle-age stomach pours over his belt, but his shirt is tucked neatly into his khakis. He has deep mocha skin traced with a white mustache. The only thing missing from his usual sideline attire is the team cap.

Why is *he* here? Coach Pearce would never attend a family function at my home. It seems inappropriate. But I guess it makes sense, since Mr. Walters paces the fence, sideline coaching Three so much during games he's basically the fourth assistant coach of the team.

"Boys, turn that nonsense off," Mr. Walters says. "The ESPN Playmakers segment's about to come on."

Bull flicks a button on the remote, and immediately, an image of the delicious Cody Knight fills the screen. Lord, does he cause me to literally clutch my pearls. We have more than a few famous football alumni, but Cody is our most elite and successful one. Before Three, Cody Knight held every record at our school that a quarterback can set. Coach brings him up at every pep rally as the person to model yourself after. But lately, he's been in the news not for his stellar play but for his sideline activism. Two years ago, Cody started kneeling during the anthem to protest unequal treatment of people of color, and his action inspired others, but then his contract wasn't renewed. He sat out for an entire year, and there was a great divide in the country over his choice to kneel. This past summer, the owner of the Carolina Panthers asked him to come work out with the team and then offered him a contract as the starting quarterback for the 2018 season. Now all the media can talk about is how he's come back stronger than ever and the sidelining didn't dampen his rhetoric at all.

"Now," says a raspy female voice from behind us, "these uninformed commentators are finally highlighting a *real* changemaker."

"Aunt Rhonda! There you are." Ray is still hollering for some reason. "I've got someone I want you to meet."

He hustles Leni toward a gorgeous woman with the same smooth, light skin as Mrs. Walters, sitting at a small table at the back of the room. She's wearing a brightly printed blazer over a maxi dress, a chunky bead neck, and a kente cloth head wrap. A new Mac and a stack of books lie open on the table before her.

"This is Aunt Rhonda. She's a professor of African American studies at Georgia State and author of the super successful book *How Black Will I Have to Be*. She was on *The Daily Show* talking to Trevor Noah about it just last week," Ray says. "You can learn a lot from her."

Hmm. Ray's an instigator, which I knew from the moment Leni told me how he basically forced this party invitation for her. I have a feeling she's getting set up again, though for what, I don't know. But this Rhonda is interesting. I've never met a prominent author.

"Rhonda, I see you're up to your old tricks," Mr. Walters says.

"Pay attention, Lamont," she snaps. "Maybe you'll learn something. Besides, as between the two of us, only one has been featured on this channel's 'That's a Scratch' segment."

Oooh, I can't believe she brought that up in front of so many people. "That's a Scratch" is a segment they run on this show sometimes highlighting sports figures who have made clowns of themselves. Last year, Three was only a runner-up in *Sports Illustrated*'s High School Athlete of the Year, and his dad went on a brutal rant about the winner that got filmed and went viral. It was a running joke on "That's a Scratch" for a week, and no one would let Three live it down. I guess Mr. Walters's family isn't going to let him live it down either.

While he glares at Aunt Rhonda, the image on-screen flips to two pundits engaged in a heated debate over the new league rule that says any player who kneels for the anthem will be fined. Everyone's trying to figure out whether Cody is going to kneel again in spite of the rule.

Mr. Walters shakes his head. "I don't see the point of what he's doing. What does he think he's going to accomplish? Is taking a knee during the anthem going to make the police stop killing people?"

"Look around this room," Rhonda says. "You have all these young minds pondering that very question. If Cody Knight is making you uncomfortable by getting on one knee every Sunday afternoon and making these pundits debate it, then he's forcing this conversation to occur. He's winning the battle that's being fought in the living rooms and on the social media platforms where these children live." She waves her phone. "He's raising awareness among people who don't experience the brutality, intolerance, and unwarranted suspicion endured by the Black community. That is what he's accomplishing."

I glance over at Leni. Her mouth drops open, and she stares at Aunt Rhonda with glitter in her eyes like she just found a unicorn. I must look the same. I can't move, I have such a crush. Over on the couch, the guys have swiveled around to look at Rhonda too. Most of them nod along as she talks, though one or two redirect their gaze, looking back at the TV or over at their coach. Three beams like, *Yeah, that's my aunt.*

I'm not the only one who notices that. Coach Brown puts a firm hand on Three's shoulder. "The sidelines is not the place for that, boys."

"What is the proper place for it?" Leni says.

Rhonda leaves her table and perches on the back of the couch. She folds her arms. "I'd like to hear the answer to that too."

"If they want to do that on their own time, that's their business. When a player steps out on that field, he's there to do a job. In no other profession could you cause trouble like that in the workplace and still have a job."

"Exactly, Coach," Mr. Walters says. "When's the last time you saw a video of a protest around some cubicles? I don't see you marching on the front line, Rhonda. Open up that computer and go back to work on your next book."

"But he's not causing trouble, is he?" I ask. "It's all the dramatic reaction to him."

"Aren't you a bright one?" Rhonda says, nodding at me. "That's my point exactly. You had a white player kneeling for years to protest women having reproductive rights, and nobody bothered about that. The league didn't impose any fines. Seems to me what we're all really riled up over *isn't* the knee. It's the man and the cause."

I can't believe I've spent this entire party outside with the boys when this queen was hiding in the corner. What a waste of my day. I also can't believe I have Ray to thank for introducing me to her. I look around and catch him leaning against the door frame. His arms are crossed, and he's got a Cheshire Cat grin on his face, like he lit a fuse and now he's watching the fireworks show. Whatever he meant to accomplish, he looks satisfied.

"Twenty years from now, are you going to remember how many yards this man ran? Or are you going to remember he's the one who stood up when it was demanded of him? Like Ali. Like Tommie Smith and John Carlos. If we're talking about career and impact, seems to me Mr. Knight has cemented himself a place in history." Rhonda gestures around the room. "What *I* wonder is what these young minds are going to do with this information. What *I* wonder is what these aspiring athletes before us would do to support their teammate if they were on those sidelines with Mr. Knight."

"These particular athletes would not do anything. The bottom line is that this is a disruption," Coach Brown says. He's not talking to Rhonda anymore—he's facing his team. "The reason for it doesn't matter. I would never allow that type of behavior in my organization."

In the middle of all this, Mrs. Walters shows up. She pushes Ray aside like a porch door. "Rhonda, what's going on in here?"

Aunt Rhonda's setting people straight is what's happening.

"We're just having an enlightening conversation." And once again, no one is a match for Professor Rhonda.

"In polite society, we don't talk about religion or politics at parties. I think we should focus our attention on my world-famous end-of-season peach cobbler, which is warming in the oven right now." Mrs. Walters looks at me and Leni. "Girls, how about I serve you first."

"That sounds fabulous, Mrs. Walters, but unfortunately, cobbler is not part of our approved nutrition plan. It's never too early to start training for Nationals."

"Now, that's an attitude I approve of. I didn't know Coach Pearce had it in her," Coach Brown says.

Leni's mouth opens like she's might actually scold Coach Brown for that insult, and I know it's time for us to go. I grab her elbow and hustle her toward the door, plastering a customer-service smile on my face. Over my shoulder, she waves and calls, "Thanks for having us!"

We don't say anything all the way out to the car. But once we're safe inside my Bumblebee, I let it out. "That was intense!"

"That was a lot of passion to display in front of a house full of guests," Leni says wonderingly.

"I'm not really surprised by that. I'm more overwhelmed that someone took down Coach Brown. Did you hear that crack he made about Coach Pearce? The nerve."

"Completely unfair," she says, then glances out the window toward the front door. "Aunt Rhonda. I didn't see her coming."

"Professor Rhonda, you mean? With her bestseller and appearance on *The Daily Show*? She is *goals*."

"What she said about supporting Cody Knight?" Leni says. "About doing something more? That was epic."

"Too right. It must have been really lonely for him to take that stand by himself."

"I've never thought about it like that."

"Watching Aunt Rhonda work made the entire afternoon worthwhile."

Neither of us has much else to say on the ride home, too busy processing inside our own minds.

9

ELEANOR

Saturday morning, we have our very worst practice of the season. Val says he's fine but looks green, and our bases miss two catches, so I have to opt out of participating in stunts for fear of another fall. Afterward, I have to shower quickly in the locker room so I can make it to Rosh Hashanah services on time. When I slide into a pew beside my mother, my hair is still dripping. She frowns at me, looking perfect in the tasteful black wrap dress she reserves for the High Holy Days. My father wears a conservative blue suit and the tallit he got for his bar mitzvah a billion years ago around his shoulders. My brother Seth, who drove down from school in Charlotte, sits on the far side of my dad, wearing his own bar mitzvah tallit. My mom isn't wearing one, but at our Reform Jewish synagogue, lots of women do, and it's super common to see them wrapped in beautiful embroidered prayer shawls for services, especially when they're called to the bima. When my bat mitzvah rolled around, my parents carried on the family tradition and gifted me a tallit. It's cream-colored linen gorgeously woven with aqua and silver threads, the 613 strings and knots, or tzitzit, representing the number of commandments in the Torah.

And it's currently sitting in the bottom drawer of my dresser at home, because I was too rushed to remember to bring it.

Great.

It takes me a while to shrug off the frustration and disjointed thoughts of the morning, to stop focusing on all the ways our team sucks this year and all the things I'm not managing to do to fix that. I can't stop worrying about what *The South Cheers* is going to say if we screw up publicly at our next game. And you know they're going to have someone there to spy on us—or "scout," as they call it. Cheer moms are something else. Even though I wish my own mother was a little more invested, I'm glad she's not like the lady who runs that blog.

The familiar flow of the service proves to be the best distraction. Hearing the congregation chant the prayers I've been chanting since I was a kid soothes my swirling thoughts. I know the words so well, I can follow along without thinking. My pulse slows. Sun filters in through the twelve stained-glass windows dotting the sanctuary, casting colorful blocks of light across the congregation, glinting off a bracelet here, a kippah bobby pin there as we rise and bend our knees and sit in unison. My eyes drift over the windows, which are art deco–style representations of the Twelve Tribes. I have years' worth of pictures of myself—from consecration, my bat mitzvah, and confirmation—posing in front of the one representing the tree, because my father insists we're descended from Asher.

By the time Rabbi Spinrad rises to give his sermon, I'm feeling as peaceful as I have in weeks.

"Shana tova, a happy and sweet new year to all. This year, I've been thinking about the ways in which our lives flow from year to year without change. Time moves on, and we're busy people. Activities fill our days, and the joys and sadnesses of life raise us up and bring us down. And that is normal and good. But on this day, as we sit together, perhaps among people we rarely see, we have an opportunity. I'd like to ask that we use this moment to take stock not only of where we are, but also of where we might go. I'd like to begin this year by loosely quoting Thomas Merton, who was quoting his mother—because we should all listen to our mothers more often than we do." The congregation laughs. "He said, 'The goal is not to see what we make of life, but to see what it makes of us.'"

I meant what I said about Rabbi Spinrad giving the best sermons. I really like hearing what he has to say.

"When I look around, both at our larger world and our

own community, I see enormous pain. I see injustice, and I find I sometimes struggle with the right words to discuss it with my children and with you. There are those who deny the humanity of people of color. Who ask that they be silent in the face of unequal, hateful, violent treatment."

An image of Cody Knight pops into my mind. He's making headline news on more than the sports channels these days. My news app sent me an alert this very morning that people have been tweeting at him that he should shut up and throw the ball, and worse. I don't know if that's exactly what Rabbi Spinrad is talking about, but it's likely, since he's both a sports fan and the head of the social justice initiative at the synagogue.

"We are silent in the face of their disparagement. You may wonder: Rabbi, what has this got to do with me? Well, I would argue that it has everything to do with us. We have a moral obligation to bear witness to injustice in society. Our tradition insists it is our responsibility to protect the marginalized and to partner with other communities to confront the powerful who perpetuate injustice. What's more, we will have to account for our actions or our inaction. To me, that is a part of our covenant. And so I ask—what will life make of us this year? Will it make of us a community that pursues justice, as we are commanded? Or will life sweep another year past the same as it always has been? To end with a quote from another mother,

Mother Teresa, 'God doesn't require us to succeed. God only requires that you try.' Shabbat shalom, and shana tova u'metuka to you all."

You don't clap after a sermon in synagogue, but from the waves of emotion flowing through the room, I bet I'm not the only one who'd like to. Yeah, I'm pretty sure Rabbi Spinrad has been following the Cody Knight news.

———————

Game day feels like the hottest day of the year so far. I know that between the last bell and when the Friday-night lights flicker on, there will be more for the team to do than we'll be able to manage. So I tell everyone to pack themselves dinner and stick around school. As usual, we spend hours getting ready for the game, working with the Booster Club to set up the merch table, painting signs, applying temporary tattoos, and putting all the girls' hair up in the squad-approved ponytail-and-bow combination. I'm drowning in sweat by the time Val, Chloe, and I put the finishing touches on the banner we made to celebrate Three's new touchdown record. I'm dwelling on the gross locker room showers I'm going to be forced to use when I feel my phone buzz in my back pocket.

Three.

What are you up to?

Getting ready for the game,
of course.

Bet you look beautiful doing that.

I glance down at my damp warm-ups.

Rn I look sweaty and gross.

Not from where I'm standing.

I jerk my eyes up, scanning the grounds, the concession
stand, the restroom area, as another text comes through.

Come wish me luck.

He stands in the tunnel leading back to the locker
rooms, wearing a pair of loose basketball shorts over
compression pants. We're too far apart for me to make
out the details of his face other than the gleam of his
smile. With his practice schedule and mine, we haven't
managed to hang out this week. I'm not sure what that
means; when Roman stopped asking to hang out with
me, Nelly said I was avoiding the signs, and she was right.
If I'd paid better attention, I would have realized he'd
moved on long before I did. But that doesn't seem like

what Three's doing. He's consistent about texting and FaceTiming me before bed.

He waves me over. I leave Val and Chloe to gather up our markers and paints and head to meet Three in the tunnel. It's not exactly private, but it's out of the traffic heading toward the locker room.

"Hey." He takes hold of the hem of my shirt, reeling me in. "Beautiful."

I wrinkle my nose. "Sweaty."

"Works for me."

"Do you practice your smooth lines in front of the mirror?" I ask with a laugh.

"You think I'm smooth?"

"You think you are."

He sets one hand on my lower back. "Is it working, though?"

It is, and he knows that. I can tell when I'm not going to win a verbal battle, so I close the last sliver of distance between us, sliding my hand up his arm.

"Guess so," he says right before I kiss him.

Three leans against the wall and holds me to him, running that hand all the way up my back and into my hair. His lips part mine, and we kiss until we're so tangled up in each other that all the stadium noises fade into the background, until we're gasping for breath. He stays close while we recover, nuzzling my cheek.

And then Bull's booming voice pops the peaceful little bubble we've retreated into.

"Three! Untangle yourself from that octopus, and let's go."

Jeez, trust Bull to be as humiliating as possible. Everyone in a fifty-foot radius probably heard that. My face and hands go tingly, like they do just before they fall asleep, and I try to back away from Three. He refuses to let go.

"You haven't wished me luck yet."

"You don't need luck, Three," I say. "You've got focus."

He grins. "Damn, you're good."

"Coach is looking for you, man," Bull shouts.

That gets Three moving. He releases me and jogs toward Bull and the locker room. He doesn't look back, but I'm not offended. I recognize when an athlete switches into game mode. Three's getting ready to dominate.

I should be hustling too. I have to shower, change, do my hair. I have my own game face to prepare and a team to hype up. But my eyes follow him all the way down the tunnel, my feet rooted to the spot where he just stood kissing me like a guy kisses someone who matters to him.

At least, I hope that's what it was.

A throat clears behind me, and I know by the sound of it that it's meant for me. I spin slowly and see Mrs. Walters standing in the shadow of the bleachers. I feel a flash of heat, wondering if she saw all that, if she heard Bull. I decide to bravado my way through the embarrassment.

"Hi, Mrs. Walters. Are you excited for the game?"

"Well," she says, looking me up and down, "I am, but I didn't expect to find my son in the cheap seats instead of getting ready."

That tingly feeling is back. I guess I don't have to wonder how much she saw or what she thought of it. "I don't know what you mean."

"I think you do."

"I know we don't know each other very well—"

"I know your kind of girl."

I fold my hands in front of me to keep them from shaking. "What kind of girl do you think I am?"

"One with an agenda. I've seen girls like you for more than twenty years, since I first started dating Mr. Walters. I watched a girl who was looking for a ride to the NFL wives suite get hold of my son Ray, get pregnant, and distract him. I couldn't stop it."

Her tone is sharp, but her eyes aren't angry. They're sad.

"So let me be clear—you should not count on my child being part of your plans, because you are most certainly not part of ours." Mrs. Walters flicks some invisible dust off the jersey she wears. She doesn't have to spin around for me to know it has Three's number on the back. "Go back to your cheerleaders, girl."

I cross my arms. "My only agenda is leading my athletes to the national championships. And your son is old enough to make his own plans."

"Athletes?" She smirks. "I predict that by homecoming, my son will have recognized you for what you are: locker-room lice."

Her smug smile sends a boiling wave of anger over my skin. She's mistaken if she thinks she knows anything about me. Her feelings toward Ray are about her, not him. And they're definitely not my problem—or Three's. I don't have to stand here listening to her insults. "You should get out there and get good seats, Mrs. Walters. Wouldn't want you to miss the start of your family's last season of high school football."

We eye each other for one more moment before she walks away.

Anger propels me through my pregame routine faster than normal. By the time I join the rest of the team, they're already dressed and hanging out in the locker room. I'm just in time for our pregame chat.

Paris is reading something from her phone. "Mr. Knight was fined an undisclosed amount for defying the league's edict regarding appropriate posture during the anthem. The team owner has stated that he will pay Knight's fine himself, using personal funds, as a show of public support for his new star QB."

"Damn, Cody Knight is all over the news for this," Kendall says.

"You know the bizarre part?" Nelly says. "Everyone is so busy arguing about what he's doing that they're not listening to what he's saying."

Her words echo like a thunderclap, the truth of them ringing in our ears. Then the team comes to life.

"Oh my God, Chanel," Gia says, "you're so right."

Sydney reaches up for a high five. "Preach it, sister."

"Nobody ever wants to listen until you make them," Trin adds.

The energy in the room spins into a tornado, whirling us all up with it. We're all chiming in, cosigning Nelly. If I stay silent one more minute, I think the pressure in my chest might combust.

"We should do something," I say.

"We should take a knee," Paris says. "In support of Cody Knight. He's our alum, right?"

I look around the room at the faces of the team. They're turned to me, eager and worried expressions mingling together. Wondering what *I* think. "I like that idea," I say.

"So do I," Nelly says. "If they won't listen to him, maybe they'll listen when all of us speak up."

"Yessssssssssss."

The hiss comes from everywhere, all of us, as one.

10

CHANEL

We have only a small window of time to get organized. If we're going to do this, we need to do it in a way that makes our point and looks orchestrated.

I stand in the entry tunnel, double- and triple-checking my bow. The excited and nervous whispers of the team jangle me. "Leni, how are we doing this? Do we go on a cue? Do we all kneel at the same time, or like a wave? What if we all go down on one knee one by one?"

"Ohhhhh, a wave," she says. "I like that. You should get them organized."

I hold up my hands, palms out. "You should do that, Captain."

"Nelly, you're the best at things like this." She nudges me around to face the team. "Please."

I go to work, because if I don't do this, who will?

"Listen up, guys. Here's what we're going to do.

Remember the routine where we go into pom-pom stands one after the other? We're going to do that, but instead of popping into pom-pom stands, we're going to take a knee. Does everyone know their position?"

"Sure do," says Avery.

"Perfect. We go on Leni's cue."

Jenni asks, "Are we all in a line or staggered?"

"In a line." I literally just asked if everyone knew their positions. I think we need a run-through to avoid a catastrophe. "Let's run it once quickly. Do pom-pom stands for now, but when we're out there, you'll kneel."

I glance down the tunnel, which is full of all the spirit squads, including the band, the boosters, the dance team, the water boys, the statisticians, the medics, and off-duty police officers as security. The football team is still in their locker room; they come out last. But the band is already playing, jumping up and down, getting us warmed up. Practicing pom-pom stands won't give away what we're about to do. We run it twice before I'm confident this will go as planned. Just in time, because then the band strikes up our fight song and runs onto the field.

Leni, Avery, Sydney, and I take the corners of Sam's celebratory banner and stretch it out so it's readable. We walk onto the field with nothing but excitement, full of adrenaline for the big game and also for what we're about to do. Everyone's energy is at an all-time high. When the band finishes the fight song, we're positioned with the banner stretched across the tunnel entrance, and the rest of the squad forms pom-pom lines flanking us. Three stands at the helm of the team, arms linked with his assistant captains, who stand on either side of him. They're all swag surfing as the band music gets louder and louder. The Ram mascot stands before him holding a confetti cannon, along with a flag bearer from the dance team.

The announcer yells through the sound system, "Here are yoooouuuur Franklin High School Raaaaaaaaaams, led by your Georgia state record–breaking captain, number three, Saaaaamuel Waaaaaaltersssssss!"

The mascot shoots off the cannon, and an explosion of blue and green glitter paper fills the air. The squad goes wild, shaking our pom-poms. Three runs forward and blasts through the paper banner, leading his team. I may not be the biggest fan of the way he's messing with Leni these days, but I can't deny he owns that field. Whether people want to admit it or not, they're here to see that boy play. He's a superstar, and we all recognize it.

The team follows him, jumping, clapping, cheering, shaking one finger in the air. The crowd is as riled up as they are. Their intensity wafts over the stands, and the roar sounds like two stadiums full of people. We maintain position and wait for the grand entrance of Coach Brown. He struts out last, clipboard under one arm, face turned down to the ground, hat pulled low, headset wrapped around his thick neck. He never acknowledges us.

The noise begins to subside as the team lines up at the benches, and we follow, finding our spots on the sidelines behind them. The band heads into the bleachers. The announcer says, "Please rise and turn your attention to the north end of the field, where the Junior ROTC squad will present the flag while the anthem is sung by Franklin High's national champion choir."

As the first strains of the anthem begin, we all look to Leni, who signals with one pom-pom and then drops until one knee touches the grass. We fall like a line of dominoes—me, then the bases, then the spotters, and finally the flyers, one by one, just as we planned.

My head is buzzing. I fix my eyes on the backs of the players, thinking about Cody Knight. It feels good to have my entire team kneeling in solidarity beside me, and in this moment, I have even more respect for him, doing it on his own.

At the end of the anthem, the team looks to me with the very obvious question of what's next. Instinctively, I nod and stand. They follow haphazardly, but I'm focused on the Junior ROTC, who stare at us with bewildered looks. They have not vacated the field as they should have by now. Their shock is the first hint that our move made an impact.

I look over at Bull, who's doing some kind of really sad *Magic Mike*-meets-touchdown dance with his famous grin, pointing at us, clearly pleased by the situation. That does not surprise me at all. Bull is always here for something out of the ordinary. His happy shimmy adds to my excitement until my eyes land on Coach Brown, who is clearly the opposite of pleased. If looks could kill, the laser beams he's shooting at Coach Pearce would incinerate her right here on the sidelines. She awkwardly claps and avoids his stare, trying to pretend she doesn't see him at all. The clapping echoes in the silence that hangs over the stands, which is abnormal for this stage of the game.

Too much time has elapsed, and the announcer realizes someone needs to push things along. "All right, football fans, let's clear the field and go ahead with the coin toss. Captains, on your marks."

Our team gets back into formation and falls into our normal routine, lighting up the crowd. Slowly, everybody around us comes out of their trance, and the game goes on. At halftime, still riding the high, we nail our brand-new routine. It's one of our better performances in a long time. I don't even take offense when Coach Pearce ducks out immediately after the game without our normal debrief.

———

My phone doesn't stop dinging for the rest of the weekend. Every message makes my heart beat faster. There's so much love and support for what we did. It's all over Snapchat and

Instagram. The squad keeps sharing posts to our WhatsApp group, and we're all totally flying. This keeps going through Monday, when the first person who greets me at school is none other than Mr. Shenanigans, Bull.

He bear-hugs me, lifting me off the ground. "Yo, I'm low-key impressed by what you did, no cap."

"Thanks, Bull." The other cheerleaders frequently get this kind of attention from the team. It's such a Hollywood-teen-movie trope, but I appreciate him recognizing me for this.

"No matter what happens, know you did the right thing."

Before I can ask what he means by that, he's headed down the hallway, high-fiving and jonesing on people, as he always does. But all of a sudden, I feel a swirl of butterflies. That comment did not come from nowhere.

"Bull!"

In the noisy hallway, he can't hear me calling to him, so I start to follow. After only a few steps, Marisol blocks my path, the streak of turquoise in her hair catching my eye, a gentle cloud of woodsy perfume settling around us. She wears a beautiful smile.

"That was one boss-lady move you pulled on Friday night."

"Thank you. I think?"

"Oh, it's a compliment," she says. "Proud of you for standing up by kneeling down."

All of the attention we've received has been amazing, but for someone like Marisol, who lives this type of activism, to say that is everything. She's done incredible things, like when she organized a bunch of different groups from the student body to create a float and march in the city Pride parade—the first time any high school around here did something like that. A helium balloon fills my chest and carries me to my first period class. I accept every high five, fist bump, and "Dope, sis!" people sprinkle on me on the way.

That balloon remains full and floaty until near the end of the day, when I receive a notification that *The South Cheers* has posted. Between periods, I take a look. There's a grainy picture of us kneeling. Of course this blog's reps were out watching our performance.

A BOLD MOVE BY THE FRANKLIN RAMS SQUAD AT THEIR OPENING GAME

This is the first time we've seen a squad take this kind of action. Does this focus on politics belong on the field? Does it take away from the experience of the fans who are just there to watch the game? Tell us what you think in the comments, Southern Cheer Champs!

Chris007: Does anyone know how the school has reacted to this? This has got to be a violation of a school code...

CheerMom&LegalEagle: Kids don't check their First Amendment rights at the door when they enter school. They have a right to make their voices heard.

RedWhiteandBlueMamaBear: These "athletes" should shut up and cheer, that's what they're on the field for— ENTERTAINMENT!!!!!!!

CheerChelsea: I'm proud of these girls—total badasses.

> **2AKaren:** Promoting ridiculous disruption? Cute. Real cute. I wonder what YOUR coach would say if she knew you were on here supporting this kind of misbehavior...

> > **BaseBoss:** I wonder what the world would think of a grown woman harassing a TEENAGER. Your own cheer days are obvi long gone—what are you even doing on this blog?????

CBT0987409734986734: They should watch out and see what "action" gets taken against them.

I knew not everyone would be on board with our decision, and you can always count on *The South Cheers* for weak commentary that misses the point but is still written with a ridiculous amount of unwarranted confidence. I wonder who's already seen this post. Some of the articles on this blog get a lot of attention. Lord, let this be one that does not. I wish there was another voice in the cheer world that could balance this conversation, but her blog is the one everyone reads.

I click it closed. I can't go down the rabbit hole of who's commenting, liking, and disliking this post.

Now I'm worried.

11

ELEANOR

After Coach sent me a text saying that some things had come up and she wouldn't be attending weekend practice, I led it by myself. Everyone was high on each other and the statement we'd made on Friday. No one squabbled, gossiped, or complained. Just like our performance, we were having our best moments together. Nelly felt it too. She brought extra oranges for snacks, set up her GoPro to take video we could study later, and spent Sunday with me perfecting the routine. Things felt like they had before my first fall, when we were the sharpest pair on the team and every head twinge didn't make me angry or worried.

Walking the halls all week makes me feel like a celebrity. I'm used to a certain amount of attention, being a cheerleader, but this is next-level. People who would normally never talk to me congratulate me. My cheeks ache from smiling.

On Wednesday, I get a text from Coach asking to meet in her office before afternoon practice, which is a little odd. Even weirder, I arrive just as Coach Brown pushes her door open. He pauses and raises the brim of his ever-present Rams hat to look at me. "Young lady," he says curtly.

"Leni," Coach Pearce calls. "Come in. Sit down."

Okay, definitely weird. I perch on a cushion on the sofa.

"I wanted to chat briefly about the team's, uh, display on Friday night."

"Wasn't it amazing?"

"It certainly was. How did it come about?"

"We were talking about Cody Knight in the locker room and how unfair it is that everyone is missing his point. We wanted to show our support for a Franklin alum. In the moment, it felt powerful. It was emotional, the way we knelt together. Everyone took notice too. It was electric."

"Yes, about that," Coach says. It's then that I realize she isn't wearing her usual perky grin. Her mouth rests in the straight line that's her equivalent of a grimace. "You understand not everyone thought that was the right statement to make, don't you? I got a few calls from the president of the Booster Club over the weekend. And I had an…interesting conversation with the administration today."

"What did they say?" My knee begins to bounce.

She considers me for a moment, then sighs. "Don't worry about exactly what they said. You have a right to protest, and I made it clear that I stood behind your decision. But the front office is anxious. They're worried about this being the start of trouble."

She doesn't normally keep details to herself, and I push my brain, which is starting to feel tired, to read the cues she isn't saying aloud. I think of Coach Brown's hard look and why he might have been in her office this afternoon. "When you say administration, do you mean the football coach?"

"He was part of the conversation, yes. He's concerned this will take the focus off of athletics."

I look down at my hands. "Is that how you feel?"

"The important question is how *you* feel. You and the rest of the team. You guys have done an amazing thing. A brave thing. I'm proud of you. I just hope you're thinking about how it will land. You must know people feel strongly about this, whether I agree with them or not."

"Of course we know that. We're not naive."

"I'm glad to hear it. I want to make sure you're all thinking rationally about it. Are you planning to do it again?"

I narrow my eyes. That sounds a whole lot like she's not in favor. She won't even say the word *kneel*. "Why wouldn't we? We're protesting injustice in this country. I can't imagine that will all be fixed by Friday night. Why would we go back to pretending everything's fine, now that we've made it clear that we think it's not?"

Coach sighs again. "Look, I appreciate your dedication.

I do. Honestly, I just wish you had let me know in advance. It was awkward for me to be caught off guard, to say the least."

A sour taste fills my mouth. Awkward for her? It wasn't *about* her. I admire Coach a lot, but she's really missing it with this response. I say nothing, and she misreads my silence, like everything else.

"Just, you know," she says, lightening her tone, "give me a heads-up next time. I'll be able to help navigate the boat better if I'm on board when it leaves the dock!"

I don't have a polite response to that, and she's my coach, so I stick with the no-reply thing. What I'd like to tell her is that we don't need her hands on the rudder. We've got this.

That night hands me an unexpected gift to make up for Coach's disappointing behavior. Three texts that he has the night off from training, and it turns out I have an empty house while my parents are having dinner in the sukkah at the synagogue. As soon as I tell him that, he responds: OMW. Bull drops him off, and I stand at the door, glutes clenched, bracing against the jerky comments Bull's likely to yell from the window of his truck. Why did he have to get a ride to what is obviously going to look like a hook-up? Couldn't he have taken an Uber?

I shouldn't care, but I do. When I spent time with Roman alone, it was fodder for basketball team gossip. He'd come over, and their eyes would follow me down the hallways the entire next day, appraising. Smirking. Judging. Nelly said Roman was the type to kiss and tell, and she was right. Anyone who thinks girls create drama but guys don't is naive. I'm not sorry I slept with Roman; I'm just mad everyone thought it was cool to slut-shame me for my choice while admiring him for doing the same thing.

I remain at the door, squinting to see Three's face as he jogs up the front walk. Tension etches lines around his mouth, and he casts a warning glance over his shoulder at the truck where Bull waits, engine idling. I wonder if he and Bull had words about the exact thing I'm worrying about. If he warned Bull to be cool. Although I wonder a little whether he's protecting me or himself, I feel safer with him than I ever did with Roman.

Bull hollers hello. "I'm going to see Paris," he says. "She'll boot me at eleven, though. I'll come back for you."

And that's it. The strain oozes out of my muscles, leaving me trembly.

Inside, Three sets his gym bag and backpack down in the hallway, making a neat tower of them. "Nice place."

I shrug. It's an ordinary front room, with a sofa we're supposed to use only for company and my grandmother's antique coffee table and credenza. But considering Three's front room has been converted into a high-end weight room/football shrine, maybe my normal is noteworthy to him.

"Want a snack?"

"Always."

I head to the kitchen for some of my famous frozen Greek yogurt and fruit parfaits. They're such a good substitute for ice cream, even my brothers eat them. I fling open the freezer and see we're down to four. This year's brutal schedule has me running low. I put a note on my mental to-do list—the one that's about ten pages long—to remind my mom to pick up blackberries for another batch. Three better appreciate what he's being offered.

He follows me into the TV room. "Mind if we put on ESPN?"

I laugh and press a button on the remote. ESPN springs to life on the screen immediately. In this house, you've got at least an 80 percent chance of turning on the TV and finding it already tuned to a sports channel. While Three inhales the parfait, I watch him watch ESPN, which is a little hilarious and a little PITA. He cannot shut up, offering commentary about every single segment. When the commentators start in on college football, his comments get personal. He played against some of these guys when they were in high school last year or the year before. He's funny right up until they start talking about a struggling freshman quarterback, questioning whether he should have been redshirted. Whether he was really ready to play.

"Better not be saying that about me in another year." He's laser-focused on the TV screen, the glow of the images flickering in his eyes. His voice is quiet, confessional, almost. Like he's forgotten I'm here. Like this is a fear he speaks aloud only when he's alone, but also one that crosses his mind every single day.

I shift closer, rest my shoulder against his, and say, "There's no space for a bad day when there's a spotlight on you."

He turns to me. Three has a few default expressions: the confident smirk he wears for the public, the pulled-straight game face he wears for football, and the worried frown he wears when he thinks no one's watching. In this moment, he shows me another face, one that is open and gentle, the corners of his mouth turned up, but only just. "Or when you wear a C on your jersey."

"Yeah," I whisper. Because I know that to be true.

The commentators drag the poor quarterback for another thirty seconds before they move on to other topics, and the air in the room grows heavy.

"Well, that got dark," he says.

Too dark. "Maybe we should talk about something else."

He nestles into me. "Maybe we shouldn't talk."

Three's lines are way less suave than he thinks, but a shiver runs down my spine. I turn my face up, and his mouth finds mine. His hands are warm on my skin, and I shift back, tugging him down so we're lying on the couch.

He freezes with his fingertips just under the edge of my shirt. "Do I gotta worry about your dad coming through that door with a shotgun?"

I laugh. "My dad doesn't own a gun."

"Okay, but is he coming through that door while I'm trying to round the bases?"

"I'm not worried. But if you are, we could put another door in the way."

He props himself up on one elbow and stares at me for a beat. "You want us to go upstairs to your room?"

"Yes. Do you?"

"I mean, yeah, but… You know I don't expect that, right? We don't have to if you don't want to."

I stand up and offer him my hand. "I want to."

———————

Three lies back, taking up my entire bed, leaving me no space and no option other than to press up against him and rest my cheek on his chest. He runs his hand over my head, ruffling my hair, which makes me nervous.

"You're not the cuddling type?" he asks, laughing.

I smile but reach over to the nightstand, fumbling for my phone. There's still time to get dressed before Bull shows up, before my parents get home. There's a chain of

WhatsApp messages from the team I should check. And I have homework to get to.

"Guess not." He takes the hint and scoots off my bed, reaching for his pants. "Just tell me you were this same way with Larson so I don't get insecure."

I freeze at the mention of Roman. Of course Three knows I was with him. Everyone knows. I don't know how to answer. Am I supposed to give details about sleeping with my ex? Am I supposed to ask him about other girls?

"Roman and I..." The words stick in my mouth, tumbling out in a weird order. "We were. Last year." Ughhhh, why is this so hard?

"You don't have to tell me," he says. But he glances at me, his eyes lidded. "If you don't want."

My stomach roils. Roman never asked about other guys. Roman never asked much of anything. We hooked up at a party at the start of basketball season last year, but almost none of the relationship happened in the light of day. Unless you count me joining his lunch table and him winking at me when we cheered at his games...which I now realize I shouldn't have counted. By prom, I was single again. If Three wants to know about other guys, if he cares enough to ask, that makes this different. Doesn't it?

"I guess you have a right to know." I raise my eyebrows, and he gives me nothing in return. "I'm the same as I always am. Don't be insecure about Roman."

"Or anybody?"

I hesitate, that trembly feeling threatening to overtake me. Like I'm about to close my eyes and crest the biggest roller coaster I've ever ridden. "Or anybody."

His mile-wide grin returns. "Same."

Whoosh.

"Hey, listen. That was some ballsy shit your girls pulled on Friday night."

He's wearing his indecipherable game face, and I can't quite read his tone. Does he mean ballsy in a good way? "You think?"

"Yeah." His dark eyes lock on my face, showing none of their usual sparkle. "Why'd y'all do it?"

"It was Paris, believe it or not."

"That doesn't surprise me," he says. He swipes his Rams football T-shirt, the one with his number on the back, from the floor, considers it for a minute, and then tosses it to me, opting instead for his plain white under-shirt. "She and Bull have been talking about Cody Knight like he's some kind of superhero. Bull's always been about the protest action, and then he fell in love with Aunt Rhonda and signed up for all these initiatives she told him about…"

A different flutter begins inside me. A nervous one. "You don't think Cody Knight's doing a good thing?"

"I'm not saying that."

"I guess the rest of the team isn't as into it as Bull. Or maybe I should say your coach isn't."

He sits on the edge of my bed, one knee crooked up so he can face me. "You shocked by that, Leni? You were there when he was talking about it. He feels it's a distraction, and he's not wrong. What's everybody talking about since that happened—y'all or the game?"

My temper flares. Is he jealous people talked more about the cheer team than his latest record? He takes up enough inches in the local news columns. But this isn't about him. "He tried to intimidate Pearce, did you know that?" He starts to shake his head, so I put my hand on his arm. "I saw it."

"Coach Brown takes this seriously."

"And we don't? He better hold on to that cap he likes to wear. This was not a one-time thing. He can make all the threats he wants, but he should know we're not afraid of him."

"Afraid? Little extra, don't you think? He's trying to protect his players. Every second counts out there. You know that. I know you do. You have to be one hundred percent focused, in winner mode, all the time. Stuff going down on the sidelines pulls you out of that headspace. I get what you're saying, I get the point, but the sidelines isn't the place to start a revolution."

I scoot away. I can't believe he's defending one coach

intimidating another over this. Especially when Brown is so obviously wrong. "You sound like your dad. Cody Knight's doing it."

"Yeah, well, Cody Knight's already got that contract, don't he? Some of us are still trying to get there, and we have a lot riding on playing ball."

"I get it."

"Do you? I can't get canceled before my career even starts."

"I don't think making a political statement should get you canceled," I say.

"It's not about making a political statement. It's about making what people think is the *wrong* political statement—and you know as well as I do that the powers that be don't agree with Cody Knight."

"You know, it's funny to pretend Cody's kneeling is a political statement and other things aren't. Even requiring the anthem to be played before a game is kind of a statement—it's a patriotic display."

"A nonpartisan one," he says.

"So is Knight's point. And that's why it was wrong for the league to punish him for it."

"I know. And yet, he still sat out for a year waiting for people to realize that. He was willing to throw away a lifetime of busting his ass. Don't get me wrong, that's real brave. I admire him. But no cap, it scares me to think about doing that myself. Fighting for social justice might be Cody's calling, and I think that's cool or whatever, but I don't think the way he's handling himself is the path for me."

Wow. Not the reaction I expected. I know how hard he's trying to make an NFL career his future, and I've seen glimpses of how much his whole family counts on him to do just that—how his parents need one of their sons to make it, how disappointed they are that Ray didn't, how they're teetering on a financial ledge trying to get Three where they all want him to go. Despite that, supporting Cody Knight seems like an easy choice to me. I'm confused by Three's hesitation.

The sound of a honking horn cuts through the quiet night. Three leans over, parting my blinds. Another honk blares. "Shit, I gotta go before Bull wakes up your entire neighborhood."

I hold out his shirt, but he pushes it back toward me. "Keep that." He plants a kiss on my forehead and takes off down the stairs.

Marisol Fuentes starts Friday morning's School Student Leadership Team meeting by pointing to me with her gavel. "I move that we amend the agenda and begin by recognizing the courageous act of the cheerleading squad on Friday night."

Her eyes skip over the students assembled, all club

presidents and team captains. School rules require us to meet once a month, and we gather in a conference room in the front office. We're supposed to talk about issues, make decisions, and guide the student body. The first year the SSLT existed, the Student Council pitched a fit, claiming they were being usurped. They weren't then, but the way Marisol runs things, they will be this year. Not that I think that's a bad thing.

"I second that motion," says Jamal Webster, chairman of the Black Social Club, "because it's about time someone showcased that kind of courage in this place."

Marisol grins and bangs the gavel on the table, the whack resounding around the room. "All in favor?"

It's unanimous.

"I would also like to take this opportunity to announce the Gay-Straight Alliance's intention to join them in taking a knee tonight."

My neck nearly cracks as I whip around to look at Marisol. She nods at me, but I can only stare. Despite my bold words to Three the other night, the squad hasn't talked about taking a knee again. We haven't said we won't, and I don't think anyone's feelings have changed, but I didn't imagine anyone else would show up with the same level of enthusiasm.

"Count us in," Jamal says.

Danny Harari says, "The Jewish Student Union will kneel."

"Girls' volleyball is yes." That comes from Londie,

who's the captain of the team. She's also Marisol's girlfriend. Marisol aims a brilliant smile in Londie's direction, who flashes an answering grin.

I suck in a breath and hold it until my chest burns. Where's this going?

"Wait, wait." Jessie Miller, drum major, holds up both hands. "Are we even allowed to do this? Will we get punished for it?"

We turn to Ms. Carpenter, a civics and poli-sci teacher and also the SSLT faculty sponsor. She clears her throat and taps one fingernail on the table. "There's no rule against it that I'm aware of," she says slowly. "I can think of instances when students have staged walkouts and the like. I know declining to stand for the Pledge of Allegiance is protected under the First Amendment."

Marisol bangs the gavel again. "See? It's legal. Jess, quit worrying."

Jessie shakes her head, her lanky hair lashing her forehead. "I don't think it's that simple."

"Why?"

She looks from Jamal to Marisol, who's leaning forward, elbows on the table. Her voice trembles. "It's disrespectful. I mean, some people say it is."

"Who're you listening to, extremists on Twitter?"

"It's not just them." Jackson Radsewicz stands, display-ing the shoulders-back military bearing he's honed as commander of the school JROTC squad. "It *is* disrespectful. When that flag is out, I'm standing at attention. Nothing less."

"Jack, it's not about the flag—"

"To me, it is," he snaps. "Find some other way to protest whatever it is you're protesting. The flag, the anthem—they are sacred."

Danny chimes in. "That's why it's so powerful for us to use that moment—"

"I'm not *using* my country's symbols for anything, get me?"

"I didn't mean that." Danny reaches over, going for a fist bump, but Jack jerks away. "Come on, I just meant I think it should be a unified moment."

"Well, it's not. I'm not even going to stay for a discussion of this topic. I'm out, and so is my squad." He grabs his bag from the floor and slams out of the room.

What a cop-out. He didn't even take the time to listen to what anyone else has to say. I think he's insulted he's not able to bark commands at us, like he does his squad. But this isn't his show. He can try to make this protest about something it's not, but that's on him. One glance at Marisol's face, and I can tell she feels the same way.

Ms. Carpenter watches him go. "I hope you all understand that this is a small taste of what's to come. Social action is never without controversy."

"But it's the right thing to do. You agree with that,

right?" Marisol demands. Her experience persuading people—adults—to take action with her comes through in every word. While the rest of us gravitate toward school-based activities, she's out there working with community organizations, like Atlanta Pride, for real.

Our teacher offers a small smile. She says nothing, but her position is clear.

"Leni, is the squad going to kneel again?"

I hold my breath. I feel Three's eyes on me. He's sitting on the other end of the room by the door, pushed back against the wall. He hasn't said a word this whole time, but he's been listening. I have a sense he's holding his breath too.

I nod.

Marisol pounds her fist on the table. "We're stronger together. GSA, Black Social Club, and Jewish Student Union. Volleyball and Cheer. Who else? Jessie, come on. Band has practically a hundred kids on its own. They're a huge block of the stands. It would be a powerful image, that whole group of kids taking a knee. Think about it. They can't come down on a hundred kids, can they? No."

Jessie shakes her bangs into her face intentionally this time. "I'll ask. That's all. I'm not going to force anyone."

A rumble goes around the room as clubs agree or offer to talk about it with their members. It's not one hundred percent participation, but there are more yeses than nos. I can't believe it. I watch kids debate and argue and agree, and I can't believe this all started with us making a decision in the locker room twenty minutes before a game. I can't wait to tell my team. They're going to lose it.

There's one last vote to be cast: the football team. Three.

"Come on, man," Jamal says. "Is football in or out?"

Three hesitates. "I'll put it out there, but I'm not promising anything."

Marisol skewers him with a look. "Are you in, though, Three? Are you?"

She's looking at him, but he's looking at me. Finally, he says, "Yeah. I'm doing it."

I think my chest might explode. He came through for me. After all that hesitation the other night, maybe something I said made an impact. He's with me. I can't wait.

12

CHANEL

Well, well, well. This morning at the SSLT meeting, Ms. Eleanor Greenberg agreed—on behalf of the team—to take a knee during the anthem tonight. During pregame prep, as I fix Taylor B.'s hair, I can't help but ruminate on that. I just think it's interesting that this is the moment she's leaning into leadership. It's easy to agree to a big gesture in a meeting, but when it comes to doing the actual work, she's struggling. She bounced in here all excited without reading the room, and her little announcement fell flat. Everyone's just standing here, staring.

Skylar folds her arms over her uniform top. "I had no idea we were expected to keep doing this."

"Yeah, man. Me neither. I think I'll bow out," Sydney says.

And look at that. You can't galvanize your troops when you've already started the charge. Leni's face turns sunburn red.

"The administration was kinda mad the first time, but we got away with it," Avery says. "Isn't it just asking for trouble to keep going?"

"Other people are going to be fighting with us this time, you guys," Leni says, sounding hyped up. "You would not believe how many teams and clubs committed to kneeling."

"What do you think, Nelly?" Gia asks.

I eye Leni. "It seems like common courtesy to ask our thoughts before making a commitment for us."

Her eyes get watery, and her shoulders droop. I'm sorry for her, but it's time Leni starts facing the difficulty of leadership.

Paris steps up to stand beside Leni. "Are you guys serious? Did you think making a woke TikTok was going to save the world? This is the real work. If you care like your social media says you do, you keep stepping up and supporting the leaders campaigning for change. If we back out now, we're just a bunch of posers. If we keep going, it means something."

A wave of relief washes over Leni's face. "Thanks, Paris."

Around us, there's nodding—some reluctant, but mostly enthusiastic. Paris has shown more leadership in ten seconds than I've seen Leni display since she became captain. But it's effective. I'm persuaded, and by the time we head out to the field, the rest of the team is feeling more confident too.

Despite the fall breeze, my entire body is so warm that I can feel sweat dripping all the way down to my briefs. The band takes its place in the stands, and the ROTC heads to the field, flags lifted and waving in the wind. Any second now. And then it's time. More eyes are on us than on the flags. Everyone must be wondering what we're about to do.

The choir sings the first strains of the anthem.

I kneel, and even though it breaks formation, my head turns side to side, watching the team and the spectators. I'm curious to see who stood by their word.

Marisol and her club have taken up residence in the dead center of the stands, and all around them are members of the Jewish Student Union and the Black Social Club. It's like a sinkhole forms in that section of the crowd. Big chunks of the band join them. Then more random people start to go down. To our left, the flag team is on their knees. To our right, a few of the ball players are down—Three, Bull, a handful of others. Not many, but enough to make a point.

I let out a sigh. We're not alone. People's integrity shows. Blood rushes to my head, and it swirls for a minute. This is what it's like when we nail a move, when we win. A smile creeps over my mouth. I've never imagined experiencing this euphoria doing anything other than cheering. All around me, people have joined us, perhaps even feeling the same way I do.

Bull's massive frame catches my eye. Most people have their faces turned toward the ground, but not him. He's looking at me, and his eyes glimmer. Is he crying? Trust Bull to show that emotion. He nods at me, and I return the gesture. Bull is the last person I ever thought I would have a moment with, but honestly, he's got me tearing up too. Next to him is another player, a white boy named Ryan, and he's not kneeling, but his hand grips Bull's shoulder like he's right there with him. His arm shakes, but he's not letting go. That connection winds from us to them to every person in this crowd who's taking a stand by kneeling down.

I'm proud of my team for leading the way, but even more, I'm overwhelmed that a large part of our community is joining together. Joining us.

If I don't stop sniveling, even my best waterproof mascara is not going to hold up.

It's not until the last notes of the song that sound from the crowd creeps back in, and I realize that the noise is not all people singing along. There's an undercurrent of hisses and boos. I anticipated that. I'm more surprised there's so little of it that I can easily ignore it. When the song ends, we all stand. Bull's bulky arm scrapes across his face, trying to wipe away the tears. It's too late. Everybody has seen. But I have time to pat underneath my eyes before anyone sees me. Well, anyone other than Bunny, who heads toward me, one hand out. I take hold of it, and she squeezes hard.

"Incredible," she says.

"Yeah, it was."

She wipes away the last trace of tears from my face with a gentle dab. "Ready to get this crowd back up on its feet? Three's got another record to break."

"Sure." I'll give her a pass on the Three fandom for tonight. I'm still flying from everything I just felt.

That feeling stays with me the rest of the game, during which Three does, in fact, break another touchdown record. To be honest, I can't quite believe he took a knee with us. Between his dad and Coach Brown, he has to know what's going to be on the other side of this game for him. I do not envy him. At least he's got this new record to soften the blow.

As we're packing up our things at the fence that separates the field from the stands after the end of the final quarter, I see her. Professor Rhonda Matthews, wearing high-waisted jeans and a flowing burnt-orange kimono over a white top. Suddenly, I think I know where Three's surprise backbone came from. Rhonda comes straight over to Leni and me.

"I knew as soon as I met you two that your passion was stronger than your fear," she says. She leans over the fence and catches us in a three-person hug. "I am so proud of you girls for speaking out. You have set a new standard for

Franklin High. Tonight, I am thrilled to call this place my alma mater."

I'm beaming. My chest sticks out, full of air, and I can barely push out a breath. "Thank you so much, Professor Matthews."

She laughs. "My sister is the formal one. You can call me Rhonda."

"Professor Matthews," Leni says, pulling out of the embrace, "did you talk to Three about this?"

Looks like Bunny is having a revelation, recognizing the thing I suspected. Three did not get here without help from someone other than Leni.

"I had a conversation with my nephew. He inquired about a few things, and I was pleased to be able to share some of my own experiences with him." She pats Leni's cheek. "But if you want more details than that, dear love, you will have to ask him if he wants to share."

Leni grins, and I wrinkle my nose. As amazing as Rhonda is, I don't care for the way she's encouraging this distracting puppy love Leni has gotten herself all wrapped up in. In spite of myself, I can't help but feel a flicker of nerves for that boy. He was braver than anyone else on their knee tonight. A reckoning is coming for him.

"Ms. Rhonda, I know this isn't my business, but I feel the need to secure an ally for Three." Leni's neck pops as she whips around to look at me. But I keep my focus on Rhonda. "Will you be riding home with him? I can't imagine it's going to be a pleasant car ride."

Her smile fades. "That's very thoughtful of you, Chanel. Don't you worry. Sam won't be riding alone. He's got me in his corner, metaphorically and otherwise. But Leni here should hit him up later. I suspect he might be in need of a friend."

"I will," she says.

"Stick to a text message, though, baby. My sister and brother-in-law are not letting him out of that house tonight." She straightens her kimono and steps back. "I cannot wait to see what's next for you girls."

"I have such a crush on that woman," Leni sighs.

"Girl, you and me both."

———

Thought I would see you at Theo's house.

> Sorry, I don't have this number saved. Who is this?

Just a girl looking for a boss lady.

Marisol. I quickly save the contact. I wonder who she asked for my number and what that conversation was like. But I am not going to ask. I don't want to risk hearing something that would derail my high. This girl might have called me bossy, but it takes one to know one. She was one of the few leaders to get the entirety of their membership to participate. I'm pretty sure there are two boss ladies in this conversation.

She sends me a GIF of Merida letting an arrow fly, followed immediately by a picture from tonight, cropped and edited with a black-and-white filter. It's the full cheer team from behind, all kneeling, plus the part of the football team that knelt, ending with Ryan, his hand on Bull's shoulder. I'm guessing she cropped out the ROTC, because the photo is a truncated panorama.

> Wow. What a moment. You captured it beautifully.

I didn't want you to miss seeing what I saw.

A thrill runs through me.

> Thanks.

The picture is so magnificent, I can't stop myself. I pull up Twitter, attach it to a new tweet, and let the emotions of the night pour out.

My Rams community, kneeling together tonight to highlight injustice. Feeling the unity as we honor our alum **@codyknight** and his fearless stand.

I go to set my phone down, but it immediately begins buzzing. I ignore it for a second, but the vibrations keep happening. I'd better check.

When I open my phone, my Twitter is blowing up. I have at least two dozen notifications and eight mentions. Most of them are my followers sending GIFs of Cody Knight on his knee and other excited messages. Then I stop recognizing the handles. People I've never heard of start to pop up. Three, four, ten, twenty—my notifications are climbing like a stock ticker. And then the root of them all appears. Jerrod from the super popular podcast *All the Smoke* has retweeted me.

I change into cozy pj's and snuggle into bed to catch up with all the missed messages and make sure I've responded to everyone or at least liked their comments. The first message I see causes me to pause. It's some grown man saying,

This is exactly what's wrong with the country now. No respect.

I go to reply, but my sister, Alana, already has.

@yaaaasAlana

No, what's actually wrong with this country is groupthink. People are allowed to have and express opinions however they want.

His isn't the only mean message. There are dozens. Alana has responded to quite a few of them, particularly the ones that are not relevant to my post but are attacking me personally. Like the people stooping so low as to make comments about my appearance. People we don't know have stepped in to help her. I craft a few responses myself and then delete, delete, delete. I want to say just the right thing, but I'm having a hard time finding the words. Every time I get ready to respond, another post pops up, and I get overwhelmed looking at the derogatory ones. The more I look, the worse they get. It's not even that there are so many bad ones; it's that the bad ones are evil. Some of them border on scary.

Should I tell someone about these? They're kind of violent. Maybe I should get my dad...

My phone rings, showing Alana's number. It's the one number I want to see in this moment, and I'm so grateful. I need a partner I can rely on to help me comb through it all.

"You okay, baby girl?" she asks sweetly.

"Yeah. I know it's just silly people on the internet, but it's still a lot."

"I'm sure when y'all put this together, you anticipated there would be backlash. What kind of talking points did you prepare for negative responses?"

Of course she would ask that. It's the basics of debate, to prepare points and counterpoints, and Alana was a champion debater. "Honestly, who thinks canned talking points could do this issue justice?"

"Please tell me that you made a post-action plan," she says. "What steps did you lay out when you initially met? I know you didn't think it would all be over once you stood up."

I release the air from my lungs. "Full transparency— this all came together right before we walked out on the field the first time."

"Chanel Rose, have you lost your mind? Have you forgotten all I taught you about ensuring you know your exit strategy from the start? *We* especially have to make sure we're two moves ahead of our opponents at all times," Alana says. "You had best get a plan now. Who was involved in this? Just the cheerleaders? Were there others? You need to set up a meeting." She doesn't even take a breath while rapping out her bulleted instructions.

"There was a meeting that included the club presidents," I say. "And team captains."

She settles. "Understood."

There's a long pause. The silence is painful. I have to say something.

"Leni and I are definitely planning on presenting a more organized front moving forward. My friend Marisol is on board and has experience with community organizing." I'm hoping this is enough to wrap up the conversation. I love Alana, but she's a lot when she gets like this. For once in our lives, I hoped she wouldn't Alana out on me.

"Well, that's good to know. However this moment was created, you've now introduced an opportunity for more dialogue about an important topic. Do the work."

"I will. Thanks for the call, sis."

"Good night."

I know she's right, even if I wasn't exactly prepared to hear it.

———

HOLY SHIT.

Marisol's text wakes me up when it's still dark outside my window.

DID YOU SEE?????

It's a surprising message to wake up to, both because of the sender and because of the content. Shouting? At 5:00 a.m.? My notifications are off. I needed a break after last night.

Oh dear God. I thought I had waded through the worst of it already. I can't open Twitter fast enough, fumbling with the phone, dropping it on my bed, picking it back up.

Get it together, Chanel Rose. Whatever it is, you can handle it.

Lord. There are thousands of notifications. *Thousands.* All linking to one tweet. From Cody Knight.

Ho. Ly. Crap.

@codyknight
Thanks **@jerrod** for bringing this to my attention. Don't underestimate the power of kids to speak truth. **#whosaysimabadinfluence**

Seven hours of thousands of strangers supporting me and insulting me and defending me and commenting on me, all culminating in Cody Knight himself retweeting me. I can't stop staring at my screen. Texts from Marisol rain down, demanding I call her, but I ignore them. Cody Knight knows who I am!

I'm bursting. I cannot believe this. In my wildest dreams, I could not imagine validation from Cody Knight. I can't help wondering who has already seen it. The first place I go, obviously, is the official YVP private Facebook group. After

I turned in my application, I found out about this group for aspiring participants, and I got added a few weeks ago. I know someone in this group must have heard about my news by now. Someone always knows the news as soon as it happens.

Of course, there's a post from one of the mods about how the program attracts changemakers. But I don't focus on that. All I can see is the third comment from the top, which says,

Can't keep this under wraps!

I hang my head. That's a code phrase, the one candidates use to direct people over to this app called Shhhhh, where they can be real. No one's going over there to high-five, that's for sure.

I hesitate. Will I gain anything from seeing what they've written about me? Alana would tell me to keep my eyes on my own paper. Leni would tell me that anyone posting on an anonymous gossip app doesn't have anything to say that's worth hearing. I'm too embarrassed to admit that I myself have commented a time or two on the ridiculous behavior of YVP applicants. Not often, just when people are really out of line. I couldn't help it… Just like I can't help opening the app now.

There are a dozen posts, all of which I know are aimed at me.

Ladies & gentleman, doin' it for the 'gram.

We have arrived at the Age of Internet Outrage portion of our program.

Lissen up, bitches, we have got an INFLUENCER right here in our midst. What's her talent? Clout-chasing.

Doesn't it piss you off when people who were never woke suddenly get woke when it involves a chance to latch on to a celebrity activist? We all know that retweet is what you were really after. Let's see how fast that activism wears off.

Wow. Instead of the Meryl-Streep-cheering-at-the-Oscars GIF I hoped to see, this is piano-dropping-on-the-head stuff. They're dragging me so hard I might develop real-life bruises. Hearing expressions of jealousy is nothing new to me, what with the clowns I see every day. But I expected the YVP applicants to be of higher caliber. These posts prove me wrong.

That sensation of flying I felt when I saw Cody's tweet disappears, and I go crashing to the ground.

13

ELEANOR

My phone explodes with excited messages. The cheer WhatsApp group is basically just a constant feed of exclamation points. I spend most of Saturday scrolling social media, and it's unbelievable how fast our picture is spreading across the internet. The trolls show up on Twitter first, because of course they would. I want to roll my eyes at the insults, but they're harsh. They're personal. They're hard to ignore. The constant stream of them drags me into a dark spiral, and my head starts to ache. That's not a good sign. I mute my notifications.

I focus instead on the texts from my brothers, Paris, Bull, old camp friends, and a bunch of other people who pop out of the woodwork.

There's one person I want to hear from who stays silent.

Nelly's warning and Rhonda's advice swish around in my head. As the noise and excitement of Saturday bleeds into an empty Sunday morning, I sleep through my alarm and nestle into the cocoon of my bed for two extra hours. The darkness from my blackout curtains is the only thing that keeps my brain from swelling right out of my skull. But it's our turn to host the rotating monthly potluck our neighbors have been having since I was a toddler. Unless I'm prepared to tell my mother about the headache, she'll fill my day with errands. The choice isn't a difficult one. If she knows about the pain, she's likely to tell Coach, who might bar me from practice. Absolutely not worth the risk.

I run from store to store with my mom's list, trying not to check my messages incessantly.

We haven't skipped a day of texting since August. Three must be in big trouble. Maybe his parents took his phone.

On my way back from a trip to Party City for plastic utensils, I swing a left into his neighborhood and roll to a stop in front of his house. The driveway is full of cars, which tells me his parents and his brother must all be there.

> I'm outside. Can I come in?

No.

The response is instantaneous. So he does have his phone. He's just not answering me.

Are you mad at me?

He doesn't respond. I should leave it alone. Rapid-fire texting someone who's ignoring you isn't a good look. My thumbs fly over the keyboard anyway.

I'm worried. Just tell me if you're okay.

Finally, he replies, telling me to wait at the playground two streets over. I speed there and pace around the swing set, probably freaking out the smattering of parents whose kids are playing on the slide and the teetering bridge. On my fifth lap, Three jogs up, dressed in running shorts and wearing his Fitbit. He snuck out?

I spring toward him, and he falls into me, wrapping his arms around me tightly. His head rests in the crook of my neck, and he stays that way for a long time. He's never held on to me like this before. His face carries no hint of the Colgate smile that sends trembles down my legs.

"You can't just show up like that. Things are hot at my house right now."

The words drop onto me like a weighted vest. "I'm sorry. Are your parents super mad?"

"They're not real happy. You know how they view any form of distraction. My mom is convinced they're going to suspend us or something. My dad is panicking about what scouts might think."

"And you?" I caress the back of his neck at his hairline. He sighs against my skin. "What are you worried about?"

"It's just a lot. Bull and you and some other kids are celebrating. My parents and Coach are pissed. Everyone's asking what's next, and I know that no matter what I do, I'm going to disappoint somebody. I'm glad you pulled up, because I been feeling alone the last day or two, but I can't lie, it isn't convenient. If my mom saw you, I'd be in real trouble."

"Rhonda said—"

"Rhonda's said enough," he snaps.

"I get that it must be tough on you right now."

"Do you? Do you know I got called in for a team meeting with Coach yesterday at five a.m.?"

Oh God. "I bet that was an epic lecture."

He stares at me. "That's all you think he did? Lecture?"

"He didn't suspend you, did he? He wouldn't. He wants that state championship as badly as anyone."

"It didn't go anything like you think it went."

"Well, what did he say?"

"That's for that locker room only. Just know that I need to get my head back in the game. No more distractions."

It doesn't take a genius to read between those lines. "We're taking heat too. The trolls have come on strong. You should see the stuff they're saying. Nelly's feed is completely taken over with hate messages."

"People are being mean to you online?" He shakes his head. "This could blow up my whole life. I could lose my offers over this. My family is counting on me. I warned you this could happen."

The blood drains from my face. "Three, everyone's mad right now, but once the temperature comes down, things will go back to normal. No one's going to hold one protest against a superstar quarterback."

"There are no guarantees, Leni. The man you claim you're trying to support? He sat out of the game he trained his whole life to play because of his protest. He *just* got back in the league. Nobody knows how it's gonna go for him. If he has one bad season, you know they'll use it as an excuse to dump him." Three lets go of me and backs away. Something inside my chest crumbles. "I've got too much riding on this. I can't take that same risk."

The sharp edges to his words and the frown on his face slice through me. A tornado of desperation whirls up through my stomach. I don't want him to walk away without saying anything more, but he's already moving.

"Sam, don't go."

"I have to get in a run. My dad'll check my Fitbit when I get back."

He starts jogging. I stand rooted to the spot, hoping he'll turn and smile or wave or something to release the tension. To let me know he's unhappy, but it's okay.

All I see is his back until he exits the park and turns the corner.

I need quiet to think about Three's words, to figure out how bad this really is for us, but my house is full of people when I return. My mother swoops down on me for the silverware as soon as I enter, then puts me to work in the kitchen setting up the potluck buffet.

"Thanks, Rabbi Spinrad," I say as the lady rabbi walks in with a dish of her famous spicy buffalo chicken dip. "How's your new nephew?"

"Sleepless." She laughs. "But everyone's healthy and happy. I'm glad I got to be there for the mitzvah. How'd Ezra do while I was gone?"

The other Rabbi Spinrad, who has entered the kitchen right behind her, widens his eyes and gives me two exaggerated thumbs-up. I grin, but before I can take up his cause and tell her how great he was, Seth turns up. I assumed he was already on his way back to school after his weekend break. The last thing I'm in the mood for is my brother and his too-big personality that fills the room and leaves no space for anyone else in it.

"Look who it is!" he roars when he catches sight of me. "Our very own social justice general!"

He links an arm through mine, jostling me. "Seriously, little sister. Way to speak up. I'm impressed."

"Seth," my mother says. "Her head!"

"Her head's fine. Quit worrying, Ma." He gives me a gentle shake. "Anyway, she can handle it. She's trending on Twitter!"

My mother frowns. "I know. I'm not sure how I feel about that."

I hate that they're talking about me like I'm not in the room. "First of all," I say, holding up a hand to stop this conversation before it runs off the tracks, "it's not about me. It's about an action we all took. Secondly, I feel fine about it, and that's all that matters."

"That was a brave thing your team did," Ezra says. "We're proud of you all. Is everyone feeling fine about it today?"

I hesitate. If I admit all that's really going on, my parents are going to freak out. "It's exciting, but it's also a little overwhelming. I don't think I—any of us—thought it would get this much attention."

Dana nods. "I imagine you didn't expect to wake up and find yourselves part of the national conversation about peaceful protest."

"Getting digital high-fives from none other than Cody Knight," Ezra adds. "High stakes, indeed."

"That's exactly why I'm worried," Mom says. "This is

a big thing for a group of high school kids to manage. And you're in a particularly precarious position. We all know the struggles you've had since the accidents. I don't know that you're ready for the fallout."

My temperature spikes. What we all *really* know is that they're using those accidents as a crutch to support their argument that cheer is pointless.

"Remind me who was protesting during the sixties and seventies, Mom. Middle-aged office workers? It's always young people." I'm channeling Marisol with that reply but desperately hope they don't push much further. I don't have her deep knowledge of social protest history. I'm repeating the headlines, but I haven't read the articles.

"Well, they didn't live in the age of internet bullies. It's different now."

I frown. "Don't make it a bigger deal than it is."

"I don't think you understand the impact this could have."

"Relax." Seth laughs. "The internet has a short attention span. Everyone's going to be mad about something else by Tuesday."

He picks up his loaded plate and heads to the dining room, and my mother and Dana follow him, chattering quietly. I spoon out a helping of dip and chips, then stand staring at it. The small ache that started at the base of my skull in the morning has crawled up to the crown of my head. I need to get this under control before I join everyone for dinner. It'll go away soon. I think. Maybe it's just a hunger headache.

Rabbi Spinrad, who's helping himself to dip, tosses me a casual glance. "Doing okay, Leni?"

I dial up a smile. "Sure."

He's good at reading people, though. Trick of the trade, I guess. "It would be fine if you weren't. You know that, right?"

I pick up a piece of tinfoil and cover a pasta dish to keep it from drying out. "I know."

"And how about your teammates and the others who knelt with you?"

"Everyone believes in what we're doing, or they wouldn't have done it in the first place." But that's not entirely true. Sydney and Gia pop into my mind. It took some convincing to get them to kneel. And obviously, Three is struggling with the fallout. Even Nelly is annoyed that I failed to consult her.

"Have I told you about the work the synagogue has been doing with Intown Baptist Church?" he asks. I shake my head. "We're partnering with them and a university professor to get faith-based organizations involved in social action. I've learned a lot by working with my fellow clergy and the members of their congregations. We've been talking about the difference between an ally and an accomplice."

"I've never heard that term in this context before."

"It's hard to define, but I like to think of it this way. An ally supports a cause without suffering any consequences for their actions. But an accomplice takes the hits along with the people they're trying to support."

"I think I get it. But honestly, Rabbi Spinrad, I'm not sure where you're going with this."

He watches me fit another dish with tinfoil, thinking for a while before he responds. "Well, as you said, this was an action many of you took. Have you checked in with the others about how they're doing today?"

Suddenly, I want to take the heavy block of worry that's been resting on my chest since I talked to Three and give it to someone else to carry, just for a minute. "Actually, to be honest, a few of us are…having a hard time. Not all of the coaches are supportive. And the stuff being said online—it's upsetting."

"Yes, I imagine it is. Very."

"But none of us discovered the internet for the first time yesterday. We all know trolling happens. This is the right thing to do."

"I can't argue with your passion or your goal. I can only share what I've learned in my own work, from mistakes I've made and will probably continue to make. It's important to listen to the people we're trying to support. Centering ourselves is the wrong way to go about doing the right thing."

"That's not what I'm doing. I know this is big stuff, but I'm not going to back down because of some internet bullies."

He nods. "I hear you. I'm rooting for you. And you know where to find me if you ever want to talk more."

14

CHANEL

As I'm packing my bag for school, my door creaks open, startling me. My mom holds the knob in one hand and her phone in the other.

"You caught me off guard," I say. "What's up?"

"So, I was tagged in something very interesting on Facebook this weekend."

I knew there was no way for me to navigate this fallout without it circling back to my mom at some point. And here it is. She doesn't have to say what it's about. This whole protest thing has finally come to her attention.

Mom holds out her phone. "How about you read it?"

A page of the *Georgia Gazette* is open in her browser.

National attention on a local football program continues. Taking a page from famous alumnus Cody Knight, a group of students knelt during the national anthem at Friday night's game. While Knight initially tweeted his support of the students, controversy surrounding the unauthorized move abounds. School officials indicated the students were not acting with permission or notification, which is contrary to school behavioral guidelines.

The cheerleading squad organized this protest last week and repeated it this past Friday despite warnings to desist from school leadership.

The Franklin High School principal made a statement assuring the community that the protest will not recur. "We encourage students to express themselves within the confines of our code of conduct. Disruptive measures like the ones taken on Friday night are out of place and will not be tolerated. We will find the ringleaders and take appropriate action."

However, students have taken to Twitter to express their pride in the protest. The *Gazette* will update this story as further information becomes available.

Oh. My. God.

In the middle of the screen is my tweet. My chest starts to close up, and my heart beats rapidly. I want to look up at my mother, but I need a moment to collect my thoughts. How am I going to explain this to her? Protesting once was one thing. This is a repeated action. And it's not the kind of action that my mother believes will get you ahead. For her, community action is about giving back through volunteering at the senior center or raising funds to build libraries in Ghana, like she does with her sorors.

My mother's voice pierces the uncomfortable silence. "Why did your father and I have to find out about this on Facebook instead of my own child opening up her mouth to let me know what was going on?"

I wish I had a vanishing spell. I'd rather be anywhere in the world than in my room with my mother right now. "It wasn't supposed to go this far."

"But it has. You left me ill-equipped to come to your aid, because I didn't even know this was happening. There are rules about how we present ourselves. The playing field is not level, young lady. You can't just do these things without thinking them through to the end. Now what? What is your grand plan to repair the damage? I have to go to a Links tea, where I am sure this will be the topic of conversation. What is it you expect me to say?"

"I don't know." I don't have the answer my mother wants to hear. I don't have the answer I want to hear. I just want to grab my bag, go to school, and get through it, then come home and head out to the shed with my makeup bag.

I drop onto my bed, and an explosion of tears bursts out of me. I'm crying so hard it shakes my bed, and all my decorative pillows flop over. I grab one and clutch it to my stomach. I know I need to calm down, but I can't.

"Baby," my mom says, sounding surprisingly gentle.

She sinks down beside me, and I feel her arms go around me. She holds me until the shaking subsides. "You really have been through it."

I'm just relieved someone is holding me up right now. I could stay here for a while.

A few minutes later, she dabs my runny mascara with her fingertips. "I can't say I thoroughly understand what you girls thought you would accomplish with this, but I believe you had good intentions. You just haven't considered the consequences that come along with things like this. Starting with this article. You have to keep me abreast of whatever fallout is happening. Right now, you need to get yourself to school. When you get home, we'll pick up this conversation so we can begin figuring out a clean-up plan."

"Yes, ma'am."

My mother backs out of my room and holds the door for me. "You're going to be late."

I glance back at my radiator and sigh, thinking of the vape bag hidden behind it. If this is how the day is starting, it's not going to get any better. But I can't do anything about that with my mother watching. I shoulder my bag and follow her toward my Bumblebee.

During the break before fifth period, I stop by my locker, though I already have the materials for my next class. What

I need is an escape from the whispers that have been stalking me all morning. Last week, random kids were giving me fist bumps. Now I'm fodder for gossip.

Friday night, I was so proud of my team and the kids in the stands and myself. The community doing that together was better than any high I've gotten out of my flowered bag. Now, every post and stare and whisper chips away at that feeling. I sink my face into my locker, searching for a hint of privacy so I can zone out for one moment. I focus on the schedules taped to the inside of the door. I just need to make it to cheer practice, and then I'll be surrounded by people who are on the same page as me. That'll lift my spirit.

I wait until the last minute of the break and then shuffle down the hallway, which is now thankfully mostly empty. I grip the strap of my bag tightly and try not to make eye contact with anyone. As the bell rings, the whispers start.

"Aw, here she comes. Thirst trapping for that Cody Knight. How many times do you think she'll check her follower count in this class? I'm taking bets."

On any other day, I have no doubt I could win a verbal sparring match with Matt Spicer, our class's Most Likely to Spend His Life in His Parents' Basement. A million retorts flood to the front of my mind, but if I engage him, am I giving the rest of the haters the go-ahead to take their shots?

"Settle down. Take your seats, we have a lesson to begin," Mr. Gordon says. "Some of us are more concerned about our grades than our fleeting internet notoriety."

He doesn't look at me, but we all know exactly who he means. I'm never the kid who gets in trouble. He might as well have thrown a dagger; even the teachers are coming for me. Should he be allowed to say something like that?

Right now, I could really use my flowered bag and a hall pass.

The intercom interrupts the awkward silence that follows Mr. Gordon's unwelcome commentary. "Chanel Irons, please report to Principal Carter's office. Chanel Irons to Principal Carter's office." There's a pause, then, "Bring all belongings with you."

The kids around me resort to a third-grade, cliché *Ooooooh* as I collect my things. I try to do it gracefully, without thinking about all the eyes on me. Nervousness over what awaits me in the office has me so shaky that I drop my pencil and then my textbook, which makes a loud thud as it hits the floor. I'm just trying to get my stuff together and head down the hall, but all of the fumbling I'm doing makes an already-embarrassing situation worse.

Matt Spicer has to take it to the next level. He shouts, "Come on, Chanel. Stop stalling and take your perp walk."

Mr. Gordon sits behind his desk and gestures to the door. "Go on, Ms. Irons."

I jet toward the office. The faster I get there, the less likely I am to make things worse with Principal Carter or run into anyone else who wants to throw darts like Matt Spicer.

Ms. Robertson sits behind the reception desk, fiddling with the top button on her mustard-colored cardigan. Her forehead folds into wrinkles when she sees me, and she offers a strained smile. "That was prompt. Smart girl."

"Do you know why he wants to see me, Ms. Robertson?" I feel confident this is related to the article that came out this morning, but any additional intel I can get will help me prepare my argument.

"I wish I could help, Chanel. I really do." Her tone is gentle and sympathetic. "But you need to go straight back to his office now."

My steps falter. That dart might not have come with bad intentions, like Matt Spicer's, but the message is clear. I'm in massive trouble.

Principal Carter's already-small office is crowded with additional people. Besides him, there's Assistant Principal Hart, who's in charge of the twelfth grade, and Assistant Principal Bryant, who's responsible for discipline. What does not make sense to me is why our school resource officer, Nichols, is here. I've seen him march out of this office with stoner kids to do locker checks.

Lord, I'm glad I did not bring my flowered bag today. Did someone tell? It can't be Marisol. She'd never.

"Have a seat, Ms. Irons. Do you know why we called you into the office?"

"No, sir. Am I in trouble?"

"Everyone in this room knows why you're here. I think you do too. Playing games is futile."

My eyes dart from principal to principal and then land on the desk, which I scan for any clues: a disciplinary form, my student file, anything. The only thing there is a bound copy of the school code of conduct, strategically placed to face me. I decide not to risk blurting out what I think it might be, possibly giving away something I might be in the clear on. Despite his investigator act, he's not going to get me to rat on myself.

"I'm sorry, Principal Carter. I honestly don't know why I'm here."

Principal Bryant takes a step forward. "You mean to tell me there are whole articles in the newspaper about your insubordination, and you can't figure out why you might get called to the office?" He shakes his head. "Rumor says you're one of our smarter students."

My head fills with white noise. Oh my god, oh my god, oh my god. Carter's mouth starts moving, and I vaguely hear him droning on, but I cannot make out any words. I look around wildly, and my eyes latch on to Principal Hart standing to Carter's right. She signed off on the after-school community service work I did last year, and she always remarks that she's so proud of me. I send her a pleading look. I know she will be the voice of reason in this catastrophe of a conversation.

Hart looks away.

"—suspension."

I straighten my back. "What?"

"Calm down," Officer Nichols says. He grips the top of the baton hanging from his belt.

This is a nightmare. I shrink in my seat and soften my voice, choosing every word very carefully. "Yes, sir," I say. "I don't mean to be disrespectful. Can I just—may I ask if I'm receiving an in-school suspension?"

"Are you trying to negotiate with me?" Carter snaps. "You got a nine-day out-of-school suspension, and I expect you will return with more respect for this institution."

I can't think of anything I've done that would warrant a *nine-day* suspension. This cannot be real. My legs are trembling, and I'm afraid they're going to give out, but I'm also afraid to move. I've never felt this alone in my life. I don't have any allies in this room. "Is that the normal amount of time for something like this?"

"For the number of violations you committed?" Bryant grabs the code of conduct from the desk and slams it into my hands. "Turn to page eight. Read the highlighted portion. Aloud."

I clear my throat. "Students may be subject to

disciplinary action, up to and including suspension from school, when they: engage in any willful act that disrupts the normal operation of the school community; engage in conduct that is insubordinate or disruptive; and/or use social media during school functions in a way that may lead to substantial disruption."

Carter begins ticking off the points on his fingers. "Disrupting not one but two football games with a misplaced 'protest'; doing so repeatedly, despite your coach being warned that you would not be permitted to continue; using Twitter to encourage violation of school rules."

They are going way too hard. I've seen horrific cyber-bullying happen at this school, and it didn't receive this reaction. They're making this up as they go along. The way they're facing off against me, there's no win for me in this room. I fear if I try to talk my way out of it, I'll dig myself in deeper. And Officer Nichols is still holding on to his baton.

I really wish I didn't, but I need help. I need to get my dad to handle these people. "Am I supposed to stay through the end of the day and not come to school tomorrow?"

"No, you will leave campus immediately. You may not return until next Friday. And that includes extracurricular activities," Bryant says, removing the booklet from my hands. "If you need to stop by your locker, Officer Nichols will escort you."

"I have everything with me." If I'm missing something,

I'll get Leni to bring it to me. Oh my God. I bet hers will be the next name called over the intercom.

Carter waves his hand. "You're dismissed."

I stand, clutching my bag, and step out into the hall, which is oddly quiet. I thought the next victim would be waiting outside. If it's not Leni, maybe Marisol? I bet she'll rage in that room, tell them where they can stick their suspension. But that vibe... I've never felt that scared before. I had no idea what was about to happen.

On my way out to the parking lot, my phone vibrates with a text from Marisol.

> Hey. Heard your name get called.
> Hit me back.

I sigh. This is sure to be the first of fifty texts, if not more, from every busybody in the school. I do not have the energy for it, so I power down my phone and stash it in my glove box. There's only one person I need right now, and that means there's only one place to go.

Thirty minutes later, I turn onto Exchange Drive and pull up to the guardhouse. I recognize the security guy who steps out. Mr. Raymond has worked here for as long as my father. When I was a little girl, he gave me my own "badge." It was just a laminated name tag, but whenever I visited my father, he pretended to scan it like I really worked there.

"Hey, little lady. I didn't see your name on the list today. Is Dad expecting you?"

"No, it's a surprise visit."

He cocks his head and studies me. "Why aren't you at school?"

"It's a long story, Mr. Raymond. I really need to see my dad."

"Anything I can do to help?"

I smile weakly. "No, sir, but I appreciate the offer."

I pull into guest parking, take a deep breath, and wait for my legs to be willing to move toward the door. I have to get out of the car and go have this talk. On the elevator ride up to my dad's office, I run through the facts in my head, trying to get them organized, preparing all the arguments I couldn't make in the principal's office. I know my father will listen, and we'll figure this out together. We'll make a plan. I'll be back in school no later than Wednesday.

My father's office sits at the end of a long carpeted hallway that leads through the open floor plan to the northern corner. A few of his long-time employees call hi, and I wave back, wishing I could disappear. I don't have the energy to engage. He's waiting for me at the door to his office, standing tall, his bald head shining under the fluorescents. His shoulders are broad under his tailored suit jacket. His lavender pocket square matches his tie, and he wears Ferragamo loafers. "What's going on, baby girl? You under the weather or something?"

"I'm okay."

"Come on in, then." He leads me into his office, and I shut the door behind us. He takes a seat at his desk. I sit across from him, dropping my bag into my lap. "What brings you to the office at eleven a.m.?"

Before I realize it, tears well up in my eyes and begin to drop. All those talking points in my mind disappear. "I got suspended."

"Suspended! For what?"

"Literally for tweeting."

"How is that even a thing? You mother told me about what the team did, but I did not think it would escalate to suspension."

"I can't believe it, either. My tweet just said how proud I was of my community for standing up for what's right. Now I'm getting in trouble."

"How ridiculous can they be?" he says. "That was a personal choice. They don't get to take that away from you."

I look at his face. I don't think I ever recall seeing him this mad. He hasn't needed to be. My sister and I are not the types who find ourselves in trouble. "I'm glad you understand, Dad. That's why I came. They suspended me for nine days."

"No. That's not acceptable." He opens the door to call to his assistant. "Stephanie, do I have anything tomorrow morning?"

I know this look. It's his impatient face, the one he wears when he's ready to move and he wants everyone to go a hundred miles per hour with him. Stephanie is organizing papers at her desk and doesn't hear him, so he repeats, "Excuse me, Steph? Did you hear me?"

"Oh, I'm sorry. Could you repeat that?"

"If I have any meetings tomorrow, shift them around. I won't be in until ten or eleven, I'm guessing."

"Yes, sir. On top of it as we speak. I don't think you have anything major."

He plops down into his seat, takes a deep breath, and looks at the wall. I see the wheels spinning in his mind. Then he looks back to me and says, "I need all of the details. Exactly what happened. Who said what. Who you spoke to. And baby girl, I'm not accusing you of anything, but you can't leave details out. I can't get surprised if I'm calling in the cavalry."

The strangest part is, there aren't any deep, dark secrets here. Everything is out there online. I took a knee, I posted about it, and now I'm in trouble. I almost wish something bigger *had* happened. I thought I was doing what was right.

I shake my head and make a blowfish face. "The only thing I did was participate in a protest. Then I tweeted about it. Different people latched on to that. Someone wrote about it in the *Gazette*. And now it's been blown out of proportion."

He reaches out and takes my hand. "I'm going to take care of this first thing tomorrow morning. Don't you worry."

I smile for the first time in hours, knowing the administration will be getting a rude awakening tomorrow when he walks into the office. "Thanks, Dad."

Leni's text comes through just as practice must be starting.

Where are you? Are you coming?

I'm not allowed. You are? Did you not get called into the principal's office?

No. What happened when you did?

I'm suspended.

WTH? G2G. Practice about to start. I am coming over RIGHT AFTER to talk.

Wait, am I the only person who got in trouble? Dozens of kids participated in the protest, and I definitely was not the only one who orchestrated it. All I know right now is that Leni and Marisol are in the clear. I bet Bull caught some heat, though. Maybe Paris too. When Leni comes over later, I'm going to need her to give me all the intel.

My dad will have me back in school quickly, though, which means I should do my homework so I don't fall behind. Instead, I take my makeup bag out to the shed as soon as I get home. Even though I normally take only one short puff, I find myself taking extra puffs today and holding the vapor longer. I need to take this escape as far as I can push it. And thank goodness I do, because by the time my mom gets home, I'm balanced. She stands in my doorway like she did this morning. "I had a conversation with your father."

At this stage, I don't know what's coming next, but I'm prepared for whatever.

"He says he has a plan. I'm going to let him work this out. I stopped and grabbed a rotisserie chicken and salad. It's in the fridge. Help yourself."

That's a surprise. I'm going to take the win and be quiet. "Thank you."

The doorbell rings, and I look at the clock on my desk. It's probably Leni, so I jump up to get the door. She grabs me in a hug as soon I swing it open.

"Nelly, tell me what happened."

I wave her into the house. "Let's grab some food and go to my room."

We sit on the floor with plates of salad, chicken, and string cheese and big glasses of water, and I relate everything the principal said to me.

"That's outrageous," she says. "It's super unfair."

"That's what I thought. Was everyone at practice? Did anyone else get in trouble?"

She's quiet. "No."

"Wow." Is this all just because of my tweet? Are they making an example of me? Or could it be because I'm Black? I've never been singled out like this before, and I'm running out of other ideas about what made my actions so suspension-worthy.

"I'm so sorry this happened. But listen, the team will stand with you. I know they'll be prepared to keep kneeling in solidarity until you can come back."

"I'm going to be back in school before lunchtime tomorrow. My dad is going to handle this situation in the morning. They do not have any real cause to keep me out of school. And *please*, don't do anything on my behalf. I don't need any more attention."

"We should do something, though, Nelly. It's not right, what the administration is doing."

"Easy for you to say. You haven't gotten in trouble for anything."

"I'm worried about Three, too, though. I'm pretty sure Coach Brown came down on him hard."

Of course she's circling this all back to that ridiculous boy. "But I bet he didn't get suspended. The whole town is anticipating the day he puts on an NFL uniform."

I thought Leni coming over would make me feel better, but all it's done is disrupt the only shred of peace I've found in this day. We finish eating in silence, and once we're done, I pick up both plates. "I'll walk you out."

At the door, she says, "I'll check on you later?"

"Fine." Good luck with that. I'm turning my phone off and checking out.

After the day I've had—after getting a suspension, which would jeopardize my chances of getting into Penn if it somehow sticks—Leni expressing equal concern for Three, whom she's known for five minutes, is unbelievable. But if I told her how much that annoyed me, she wouldn't even get it. She loses her focus the minute some boy comes around. When she was dating Roman, she practically had her wedding dress picked out. And here she is, doing the same thing again.

I'm looking forward to a new day tomorrow.

15

ELEANOR

Nelly is not back in school on Tuesday. Or Wednesday. In fact, the administration puts its foot down, and despite all the pressure her dad brings, they refuse to reverse her suspension. A schoolwide email goes out talking about insubordination and disruptive conduct. *It has come to our attention that certain students...* Another one goes out to the SSLT immediately afterward: *As our most prominent student leaders, we expect you to set an example of behavioral standards...* They both end the same way: *Behavior that violates the student code of conduct will not be tolerated.*

Neither of these missives mentions Nelly by name. They don't need to. We can look past the administrative jargon veiling the threat and the target. The warnings set off a debate among the student body. Some people argue that we have to keep kneeling to prove our point. Others pretty loudly insist that we never should have done it in the first place. Kids with lawyer parents offer to involve them. Others don't want to risk getting in trouble. Arguments can be heard in every hallway and at most lunch tables all week.

We reach fever pitch on Friday. The school always buzzes with anticipation the day of a game. We're playing away tonight, which means we'll be boarding a bus right after school to drive to our opponent's field. We can't stop talking about how things are going to go down tonight.

"Come on, you can't ignore the fact that the only person who got in trouble just happened to be a Black girl," Marisol says. She and Londie have been sitting with us at lunch since we knelt. My heart squeezed a little when she mentioned earlier that she'd been texting with Nelly. I haven't heard from her since I went over to her house. I haven't actually heard much from Three, either. It's not so bad that I'd call it ghosting, but it's close.

"Exactly," Bull chimes in. "She got played."

"This ain't nothing new," Paris adds. "I bet that office became an interrogation room. So the question is, what are we going to do now?"

The entire table looks to me.

I am the captain of the cheer team. I should have an opinion about what to do. I really don't want to say we should back down. I'd feel like we would be letting down...I don't know, everyone. Why would we give up now? But a teeny voice at the back of my head keeps replaying Nelly, telling me not to draw any more attention to her, and Three saying he's worried about college offers.

I don't know what the right thing to do is. And I've got only a few hours left to decide.

The bus rides to away games are usually pretty boisterous, with hair styling and temporary-tattoo application and battles for playlist dominance. But we're subdued today, holding quiet conversations with our seatmates instead of shouting from the front to the back of the bus. I sit alone in a seat near the middle and participate in none of the discussion, feeling the brush of every glance that flickers my way. I wish desperately that Nelly were sitting beside me. That I could ask her what to do.

How am I supposed to captain at all without her, let alone make *this* choice?

I consider sending her a text, but she won't answer. I know if it were me, I'd be horrified I was missing a game over a suspension. I don't want to make her feel worse by rubbing her face in the fact that she's not here. So I put my phone away, put my earbuds in, and try to distract myself with music. There's not enough volume on my phone to drown out my thoughts, though, and the bus arrives at the other school before I'm ready.

Our downcast mood carries over to our locker room preparations, which are quick today, since we arrived suited up. Because of that, we're allowed to make our locker room coed. I still don't know whether I should tell them we're kneeling again. The tension weighs on us all. A couple of bickering sessions break out, and I feel a headache begin.

The moment for a decision is coming.

I'm lost.

As we hear the home team band begin to play some pregame warm-ups, loud knocking on the door makes us all jump. A deep voice yells that everyone better be decent, and then Principal Carter barges in. Coach Pearce dogs him, practically stepping on the heels of his shiny loafers. Everyone freezes. The principal has never—not once in my almost four years at Franklin—made a pregame locker room appearance. Not even when we competed at State. Somehow, I have a feeling he's not here to give us a pep talk.

"Squad—er, Team," he says, planting himself in the center of the room. "Your attention, please."

A couple of people file over from the bathroom area, where they were doing last-minute hair and lip gloss checks. Paris, who's been stretching on a yoga mat in the corner, folds her body into a crisscross-applesauce position, her face turned toward the principal. I sneak a peek at Coach Pearce, who's avoiding my eyes. Her face is pink, like maybe it was recently red and is still fading back to normal.

Carter looks at us, settles his face into a grim mask, and

says, "I'm here to let you know that you will be remaining in the locker room for the pregame program. You may come out once the first quarter commences."

Silence follows his pronouncement as we work out that he means we have to stay in here for the anthem.

A frustrated murmur swells among my teammates. I step forward. "Is this decision only for tonight's game?"

He glares. "The rule applies going forward at all school sporting events."

"But the cheerleading team is always on the sidelines," Paris says. Her comment opens the faucet, and everyone else's mumbled complaints spill out.

"Even for homecoming?"

"Who's going to form the tunnel when the team takes the field?"

"Will the opposing team have *their* cheerleaders on, but not ours?"

We all talk at once, creating a reverberating cacophony of sound in the poor acoustics of the tile locker room. The twinge behind my eye that started on the bus grows into a full ache.

Carter holds up his hands, warding us off. "This decision is final." His voice rings louder than any of ours, and the color rising up his neck matches the angry shade of Pearce's cheeks. "No further disruptions will be tolerated."

"Coach?" I say.

She folds her arms across her chest and frowns at Principal Carter. "Unfortunately, Leni, my hands are tied. But I want it to be clear that I don't like this."

I finally connect the dots that start with the little visit Coach Brown paid to her office. The old boys' club is ganging up on her. "Are any of the other pep squads being kept off the field?" I demand. "Or just us?"

"This is the measure we deem necessary, Ms. Greenberg," Carter says. He's dodging my question, but that's answer enough. "Your coach will call for you when you may join us on the field."

With that, he turns and exits. The door swings closed behind him with a resounding thud, and we're left to stare at one another blankly. I should say something. I don't know what, though. The distant sound of a band playing signals the start of pregame just a few hundred feet away on the field.

"Coach, you know this isn't right," Paris says.

"Are we just going to let them bulldoze us?"

Coach Pearce sighs. "It would be insulting to you all to act like this is fair. It's not. And you're right—no other club or team is being punished. They're making an example of you. However, as I said, there's a lot of bureaucracy around this decision. I can't just reverse it, much as I would like to. I'll chip away at it, and I'd like you to trust me to work on your behalf. But we're a team, and I need you not to make any decisions without me. That would make it much harder for me to protect you."

Good. Finally, a teacher who gets it. I clap my hands once. "Okay, Coach. We can work with that."

She leaves to monitor when the anthem ends so she can signal us to emerge. For the remainder of the pregame, no one in the locker room breaks the silence or the tension we stew in.

After the game, a few of us gravitate to Bull's basement. His friends from the team end up here most Friday nights, and some of the girls from the squad, too, though it's my first time. There's a man-cave feel to the basement, between the big-screen TV, the front-and-center video gaming system, and the pool table. Which makes sense, given that when we walked in, Bull's dad and a couple of other guys his age were hanging down here. They cede the space to us, but not before returning a bottle of whiskey to the liquor cabinet in the corner and padlocking it.

We don't arrive together, but Three catches hold of me at the bottom of the stairs. "Hey."

"Great game tonight," I say, feeling a little thrill. "That was an amazing pass in the fourth. Of course you made that throw."

He grins, turns my chin to kiss me, then grabs me by

the hand and guides me into the basement. He's been so chilly lately, I wasn't sure he was going to pay attention to me tonight. Playing hot and cold like this gives me whiplash, but I've been missing him, and I'm not going to turn it down.

Bull's phone is connected to the sound system, and there's a trap playlist thumping in the background, but not so loud we can't talk. A good thing, since we can't seem to shut up.

"It's bullshit, is what is it," Bull says.

"That part," Paris says for about the fourth time. She and Bull have been the most vocal. "No one else got banned!"

"You did start it," Three says. He's sitting in one corner of the worn leather sofa while I perch on the armrest beside him. One of his elbows rests casually on my thigh, but otherwise, he's not touching me. In contrast to Bull, who's got Paris in his lap in an armchair. Also, Three's the only one whose mouth hasn't been running a hundred miles an hour.

"Hell yeah, they did," Bull says. "No one else had the balls."

Three flips open the top of his water bottle, which is filled with one of those recovery shakes his dad makes him drink. He flips it closed again without taking a drink. Then open. Then closed. "I'm just saying, they gotta be prepared for the consequences of their actions."

Their? Doesn't he mean *our?*

We've been dealing with the consequences for a while now. I pulled up Twitter briefly while Bull drove us to his house and saw that the trolls had been busy. We weren't trending anymore, but there were thousands of tweets about us—some supportive, others not. Many were nasty, full of slurs and threats. And there was a new thread, rapidly gaining likes, with a grainy close-up of Nelly and me kneeling that said, *Now we've got a Jew bitch on her knees with the primates.*

Seeing that was a gut punch. I closed the app fast, wondering how they knew I was Jewish. Did they dig through my old posts and see references to youth group? Or maybe my last name was enough to trigger those types.

I take a quick breath, pushing aside those thoughts. Those are anonymous strangers on the internet. Cowards hiding behind screens, using their keyboards as weapons against kids. But our own school trying to scare us into silence? That's different.

"We shouldn't be scapegoats," I say. "Carter's the one who's trying to punish us. Shouldn't he—and the administration—at least listen to what we're trying to say? Freedom of speech and all that."

"I don't think it works that way in schools," Gia says. "I think schools are allowed to prohibit disruptive behavior and it's not considered an infringement on our rights."

"That's that bullshit I been talking about," Bull says.

"The only people disrupted were the ones who are too scared to acknowledge the truth."

Bull's words electrify me. "Exactly," I say, nodding in his direction. "This isn't really about disruption. It's about shutting us up. There has to be something we can do."

"Like what?" Gia giggles nervously, looking from my face to Bull's. His broad smile gleams, and sweat beads at his temples. His excitement is palpable. I wonder if I look the same.

"I don't know. A...walkout? Or a sit-in, maybe. Something to make them pay attention to what we're saying. You know who'd have some ideas?" I snap my fingers. "Marisol. Or, no, Three's aunt Rhonda! We should get her involved."

"Yo, hold up," Three says, lifting his elbow from my leg and leaning back. "Do. Not. Call. My. Aunt."

"Come on, Three. She'd be a great resource to help us navigate the trouble."

"No, Leni. I'm asking you to leave her out of it. I would also rather not have this conversation right here, right now."

I lean toward him and set my hand on his shoulder, massaging it gently. "But a collective action—"

"We take a knee, and they start handing out punishments. You think we're not going to get hit if there's a walkout?"

"What are they going to do, expel *all* of us?" I scoff.

I glance around, expecting solidarity from the rest of the group. But most of them wear awkward expressions and are looking around at the walls, down at their feet, anywhere but at me. Even Bull shakes his head and gives me a cautionary glance. But I know they'll come around with a little encouragement. "When we—"

"What *we?*" Three snaps. "I'm not walking out. Some of us have a lot to lose."

"We all do," I say. "That's kind of the point."

"We're not all gonna have the same consequences."

"What are you talking about?"

He looks up into my face, eyes like lasers, mouth flat. "How come your girl got suspended, but you're still in class, still on the sidelines at the game, still sitting here talking about walkouts?"

"It's because she tweeted—"

"You think that's why? Your whole squad did this thing. You're the captain. How come they didn't come down on you? How come she's the only one?"

I blink. Yes, it was a group decision, and I am the captain. But I didn't tweet about it. That made a difference. Didn't it? They are making an example of her, but doesn't that make it more important to fight back?

Three's not done. He moves my knees aside to make space for himself to stand. "You ever think about why you got named captain? Why your coach picked you? You sat on that bench all last year, injured. Chanel carried that team. And yet, when it came down to picking captain, somehow it wasn't her. Why do you think that is?"

"What's that supposed to mean?" A bowling ball rolls into my stomach and settles there. "Are you saying I don't deserve to be captain?"

"I'm saying you never even asked yourself the question. I'm saying you're over here talking about civil disobedience, knowing they're going to be gunning for us, and you're not even thinking about whether your friends are wearing the same size target as you or whether you have armor that we don't."

He's so far out of line. I stand, too, and somehow we're facing off. "I don't know how this became about me."

"I think it's been about you the whole time."

"That's not fair," I say, my face warming. The whole group has fallen silent. Bull's phone has reached the end of the playlist, and I guess he didn't set it to loop, because the music is gone too. It's just Three and me and a toxic cloud of anger swelling between us, poisoning the air, and everyone watching it happen. "I don't agree. I just want to do what's right."

"No, what you want to do is put on a show. You don't appreciate how hard you're making this on some of us. You're putting us at risk, but you're not risking anything."

Absolutely. Not. True. He's mad right now. He's not

thinking through what he's saying. He just doesn't like attention he can't control. "You're wrong."

He shakes his head and grabs his bottle from the side table. He appraises me for a second, unblinking.

I don't want to keep fighting in front of everyone. And clearly, he doesn't either. "Let's take a beat," I say. "I'm going to grab a LaCroix."

I head for the basement fridge. Paris follows me and touches my wrist gently. She and Bull are famous for their public displays of drama, so she must get how humiliating this feels. She glances back at the boys. Three's heading over to play pool with Bull, a look of sheer exhaustion on his face. "Paris, can you give me a ride home?"

"Yeah, bae. Let's go." She pulls out her keys, calling to Bull, "Hon, we're taking off, okay?"

"Come over here and give me some sugar before you go." She gives him a peck and then heads back toward me and the stairs. "Drive safe, baby," he calls after her.

I'm tempted to do the same with Three, but when I catch his eye and he gives me a reluctant, "See you later," I know it's not welcome.

I'm out the door before I even process what just happened.

16

CHANEL

The last night of my suspension, I'm in my safe space. Unlike in most people's garden sheds, my mother refuses to tolerate any level of filth. She had this place custom outfitted by the Container Store, complete with shelves and a wooden workbench. I normally gather up all my trash and tuck my stash away in my room, but since the suspension, I've accumulated an unfortunately large pile of cartridges, and I've been careless about getting rid of them. I'd count them, but it feels unnecessary. It can't be as many as it looks like. If someone came in right now, I guess I'd finally have to have a conversation about my relaxation method.

My mood right now is pretty similar to the way it was the night Leni's brother, Seth, introduced me to this method. A few weeks before State last spring, things were looking really rough. Our pyramid was not in shape, and the flyer who had replaced Leni at the top could never stick her stunts. Leni's pain back then was so severe, she couldn't even come to practice to watch, and I had absolutely no support. Kind of like right now. I wound up at her house one night despite that, just needing to blurt out all my frustration to someone who'd understand. Leni had been out, but Seth had been home. He'd listened to me have a near panic attack and then gifted me my first cartridge.

Now, with as much time as I've spent in this shed recently, I realize I'm falling behind. I know I need to get back on top of my life, but I'm struggling to find the motivation, and that doesn't feel like me. I've spent the last couple of days trying to catch up. I glance at the vape pen and decide I'm going to put it away. Tonight I need to plow through the last bit of work so I'm ready for tomorrow.

I decide to spend some time looking into the impact of this suspension on my plans. According to the Penn website, a disciplinary action on my record would definitely be grounds for them to reject me. Early admission was my original goal, but now I'll have to wait to apply until hopefully we can get this cleared off my record. I'm starting to worry I'm going to miss all the early action deadlines. And that's assuming my parents can get this cleared at all. I'm nervous that if they can't, I'll have to report it to YVP too.

I just need to be prepared so I'm not caught off guard by another disappointment, like my dad coming up with a complete goose egg on getting my suspension reversed. I sat in the hallway, ready for it all to be cleared up so I could head to my first-period class. When he emerged forty-five minutes later, he gave me a strained smile that could not hide the anger in his eyes.

"Dad, what happened?"

"Come on," he replied. "We'll talk in the car."

I knew that meant I wasn't going to class. My bag weighed a million pounds on the walk back down the hall and out of the school. In the car, he told me they had flat-out refused to lift the suspension, no matter how he argued. Finally, just before they'd left the room, he'd told them, "If I dig deeper and find there have been similar infractions that resulted in lesser punishments, this school will be in for a rude awakening."

As he drove me back home, he turned on the classical station, and I knew that meant he was thinking, just as I do. His distraction gave me a chance to turn my face toward the window and let my tears fall.

Two weeks later, the suspension is finally ending. I'm about to face everyone at school tomorrow.

One of the few lights during this dark time has been my friends. Not Leni, who I have not been in the mood for. But Bull and Paris and a few others have reached out to check in, give me homework notes, and make sure I know they're containing the rumor mill and that everyone is on the same page about my suspension being too harsh a punishment. I even heard there was a spirited debate that ended in my favor in a poli-sci class.

Just as I'm reflecting on how surprisingly supportive they've been, Val calls. I'm so shocked to see his name, I answer on the first ring.

"Hey, girl. Ready for your big comeback tomorrow?"

Big comeback? Dear god. I just want the day go as if I've been there the whole time and the whole suspension thing never occurred. I want to fly way under the radar. "I'm hoping it's the dullest day of my life."

"I don't anticipate that being the case. Child, you have been the center of the conversation since the day it happened. And since when have you not wanted to be the center of things?"

"Not like this!"

"Clout is clout, no matter what form it comes in," he says. The bounce in his voice both excites and comforts me. I may not completely agree with that sentiment, but if Val is behind me with this level of confidence, then even with all eyes on me, maybe the day won't be a total horror show. "Don't worry, I got your back. Meet me by the lockers in the morning."

I smile. "I would absolutely love that. See you before first period."

That phone call makes me feel a whole lot better about what I'm walking into tomorrow. He may not even know how much I appreciate that gesture.

During my first few weeks back at school, the tension comes and goes. I definitely have my supporters, who voice their anger over the excessive punishment, but that doesn't negate the haters, who spout their opinions in class debates and in the hallways, making sure I know they think I'm in the wrong. Some of those voices belong to the faculty. I power through by focusing on cheer. I'm always so relieved to walk into practice, which has become the one place I know people will be on my side. In the past, it's been the place I've faced the most opposition—not everyone agreed with my suggestions for how to improve the squad—while the classroom was the place where people let me have the floor and my leadership was appreciated and welcomed. Now, like everything else in my life, it's upside down, but I'm grateful to have somewhere I can relax.

My teammates avoid the subject of my suspension, like they all know I want practice to feel normal. I'm finally able to share more of what I learned at camp, things I never got to teach the team because of what a debacle this season has been so far.

We're all getting along just fine, until one practice when Leni calls for us to practice our pregame routine, and we devolve into a mess.

"I'm sorry, does anyone want to practice a routine we can't actually perform?" Natalia says.

I was definitely thinking the same thing. But for the first time, someone else gets to be the bad guy.

"Well, we still need to practice it." Leni folds her arms. "You never know what could happen."

"Maybe next year," Skylar says. "But this year? Not. Happening."

Kendall adds, "Actually, can we talk about the plan for the rest of the day? These practices have been all over the place lately."

Leni clenches her fists.

I can't help but jump in. "This routine is good warm-up. We should run practice like we normally do. Let's work on some sideline cheers and our halftime routine and close out with our routine for Nationals."

Val applauds. "All right, the boss bitch is back! Never thought I'd miss the drill sergeant, but at least we have some order again. People, let's get started."

It took my life going completely haywire for them to finally see that all I was ever trying to do was bring some focus to the team. Feels good to be understood for a change. I bury a smile because I don't want to gloat. Leni's eyes are on the ground, and she's taken a few steps back. Poor girl—Val's comment had to sting. But this is what being captain is. If she wasn't prepared for it, she had the opportunity to express that to Coach. She didn't. That means she has to endure the consequences of her decision.

In the end, it's one of our better practices in a while, even though I can't make it through ten minutes without a coughing fit, which has happened quite a bit since I came back from suspension. It's starting to attract the team's attention; Coach studies me, and Val asks if I'm getting sick. Maybe all the time I've been spending in the shed behind my house is catching up with me. I can't keep going like this.

Friday afternoon, we sprawl on the lawn by the field, enjoying our pregame snacks. The upbeat vibe from our last few practices is no longer present.

Jenni plays with her carrot sticks. "I'm not enthused for games anymore."

"Me neither. You can feel the cloud hanging over us. People don't even really clap for us when they finally let us out of locker room," Skylar says.

Coach Pearce, who's been sitting and eating with us, claps her hands. "Gather in, Rams." We scoot closer together. "We can't become so wrapped up in this one little thing we're not able to participate in. We still have State and Nationals, and we are going to crush it. We're going to show everyone who tried to hold us back this year that we're still an elite squad with amazing routines. Despite the disappointment of the past few weeks, we must find a way to convert our energy into a winning spirit. Otherwise, what was it all for?"

Okay, that's right. That's something we can work toward. That's something that has a formula I'm familiar with. I can't guarantee a win for us, but I know what we need to do to work up to it. I feel a sense of relief, being able to focus on this.

The squad is sprawled out on the itchy grass, but I'm on my pop-up stool. As they gather up the remains of the snacks, I fold up the stool and store it in its purple canvas satchel. Leni has finished only half of the snacks she's brought. She's been withdrawn all week, her stress on display in a frown she normally wouldn't show anyone but me. I hate to see it. I can't remember the last time she let something get the better of her this way. It doesn't happen frequently. When it does, it's a big deal. Leni does not allow frivolous things, other than the occasional boy, to disrupt her psyche.

But losing the respect of the team wouldn't feel frivolous to me, either. We've worked so long and so hard to be leaders, starting with the time we ran for president and vice president of the fifth grade. Taking a step back is not something either of us really knows how to do.

Part of me wants to comfort her. I can't help but think that's not my job, though. Not anymore.

———————

Throughout October, my focus is split between two things: getting our competition routine solid, and working with my parents to get the suspension removed from my permanent record. I've been waiting to ask my guidance counselor, Ms. Murphy, to complete all her responsibilities for my early action application until we see if we're successful. But now that the deadline is close, we have to have a conversation with her about what to do.

My parents wait for me outside Ms. Murphy's office. "Hi, Mom. Hey, Dad."

They respond by standing and giving me hugs. My dad flashes me a bright smile, the same kind he gave me when I was learning to ride a bike, fell off, and skinned my knee. He told me, "First, fall down. Now, riding is next."

The door swings open, and Ms. Murphy greets us and waves us into her office, where she returns to her exceptionally neat desk. Other than the media specialist, she's the only teacher who has such a large collection of books in her office. There are college guides, SAT/ACT prep manuals, a display shelf with face-out pamphlets about depression and anxiety, and a shelf dedicated to fiction.

I focus on Ms. Murphy, who speaks first. "Hi, guys. Nice to see you all. So, I did read your email, but why don't you reiterate what exactly we're discussing today?"

"I'm disappointed it's come to this," my dad says. "As you know, this is not my first attempt to address this situation. I tried going through the other channels, but things still haven't been resolved as they should be."

Oh my goodness. My father is a strong personality, and sometimes it's a lot. I hope Ms. Murphy does not take this the wrong way. This is my last effort to rescue my academic career. We do not need to antagonize the guidance counselor when we're depending on her for some help. Considering the hard work I've done all these years to get where I am, the fact that we're even having this conversation is just so unexpected. I never thought I was on a path that could lead here.

"Have you heard anything about the appeal? Have you been given any indication if it's looking good or bad?" Ms. Murphy asks.

"Our attorney thinks that based on Chanel's stellar academic and behavioral record up to this point, we have a very good chance of having the suspension removed from her permanent record," my dad says. "Further, an audit of punishments handed out at this school revealed that on no other occasion did a student's exercise of their right to protest in a manner that did not disrupt classes receive such a long suspension. The lawyers are confident we'll be able to show Chanel was unjustly singled out for an unusually harsh punishment, and I am too."

I look down and notice my mother give my dad's hand a little squeeze. He glances at her, and they lock eyes for a second. I've seen that squeeze before. Although my dad wouldn't harm a fly, his stature and his tone when he gets excited can seem intimidating to white people. He takes a deep breath, and when he speaks next, I notice his voice has softened. His proud posture deflates, as it does whenever he is forced to unfairly censor himself in the presence of white people.

"Listen, I'm just trying to make sure that a child who has worked harder than I ever could have imagined—a kid who has never needed motivation from anyone else—doesn't have her academic career threatened. It seems like there must be a more just solution."

Ms. Murphy scoots her chair closer to her desk and leans in, almost as though she wants to make sure no one listening outside her door can hear what she's about to say. "Nelly has been one of the bright spots in my time at this school. You are exactly right. She is self-motivated and smart and obviously gifted in academics and sports. However, my hands are tied. I have to send them everything that's in her file. I suggest we wait it out and hope the administration does the right thing. If it does, I'm not obligated to say anything about the suspension."

My mom pipes up for the first time. "Then I guess we wait."

And there we have it—I'm going to miss the early deadlines. This is a disaster. I just knew Ms. Murphy was going to have an answer for me. She's one of the smartest people in this building. If she can't figure out a workaround for me, who can? We've got one last-ditch effort with this appeal. If that doesn't go well, I'm concerned about my chances of getting in anywhere.

I stand up quickly. I can't spend another second in here. It won't be useful to me, and it will just keep reminding me of the *no*. "Thanks for seeing us, Ms. Murphy."

"Anytime. If there's anything I can do to help, please let me know."

This meeting was literally about seeing if you could do something to help. But whatever.

———————

A week later, a letter arrives from the Young Visionaries Project. I sit on the edge of my bed, twirling the envelope in my fingers for a ridiculously long time. Three months ago, when I discovered the program, I felt fully confident I would be a member of this cohort. I don't feel that way right now. Once I open this, I'll know. There will be no turning back.

The other applicants on the Shhhhh app are merely my peers, and the way they dragged me shouldn't matter. Even though it's a bad idea, I've continued to check the app over the last month, so I know two things: one, they have not stopped dancing on my grave, and two, some kids have already gotten in.

If Alana were here, she would have already ripped this envelope from my hands and given me a great pep talk about how amazing I am no matter what's inside. I could FaceTime her. But the idea of reading a rejection aloud is mortifying.

I think about calling Leni. She's the one person I've

never been afraid to let see me in the raw. Val and Paris are great, but we're not connected in the same way. I don't have a desire to open that door with Leni yet, though. She's probably busy with Three, anyway.

I take a deep breath and slide my letter opener—the mahogany-handled brass one my grandfather left me—across the top of the envelope, ripping it open.

Dear Ms. Irons,

We appreciate your application to the prestigious Young Visionaries entrepreneur program. As you know, we receive tens of thousands of applications for a very limited number of spots, and this year, our applicant pool was even more impressive than in past years. Unfortunately, we are not able to admit all applicants, and we regret to inform you that your application was not accepted. We know you will continue to follow the program and cheer on the cohort that was chosen. We wish you all the best in your future endeavors, and we are confident you will shine in all you attempt.

I tear the letter in half and then tear it again and again until I've shredded it into a pile of confetti. I snatch up all the shreds I can hold in one hand, pull my flowered bag out from behind the radiator, and march into my bathroom. I flick on the fan, pull my lighter from the bag, dump the remains of the letter into the sink, and set them on fire.

They go up with a *whoosh* but singe quickly, so I turn the water on to douse the flames and wash the remains down the drain. A small scorch mark lingers in the sink even after they're gone. I check inside my flowered bag, and thankfully, I have a few cartridges left. I should have time before anyone gets home. I lower the toilet lid, take a seat, pull out my vape pen, and press the button. The layer of stress that had settled on my shoulders lifts off of me. I take out the lilac-and-lavender-scented aromatherapy candle I bought online and light it. Then I sit there.

It's nice to let everything just be.

"Chanel Rose!" My mother's voice rings out.

Oh my god. Did the smell seep downstairs? Why didn't I go to my shed? I pull out an air freshener, spraying wildly, even getting on my knees to spray the crack under the door, and then scramble to get everything zipped back up in the flowered bag.

"Yes, Mom?"

"Put something decent on, then come downstairs. Your dad is taking us out for dinner tonight."

I don't want to be trapped in the car with them while I'm high. "Do I have time to take a shower?"

"No, he said he's two minutes away. Come on down."

I definitely need a plan, but I'm moving in slow motion. First things first. Clothes off. I head into my room and grab the first thing my hand touches in my drawer. I struggle to pull on the tights. Why did I think I could get tights on right now? But there's no time to change course at this point. I take my gray sheath dress from the closet, toss it on, and run down the stairs, hoping the rush of wind will remove any remnants of my recent activity.

The front door is open, but the screen door is closed. It looks like Mom has already gotten in the car. I fumble for my keys, lock the door, and take a second to check myself out. I take a whiff of my dress, and all I get is a strong scent of fabric softener. Okay, I'm straight.

But as soon as I slide into the car, my father sniffs loudly. "What is that smell?"

Oh, fuck. I freeze. Maybe he's talking about something else.

They both turn around and look at me. Dad leans way into the back seat and inhales deeply. "Have you been smoking marijuana?"

"No," I say.

"You don't think we know what weed smells like?" Mom says.

I'm too high to come up with something other than, "I would never do that!"

"Everyone out of the car," Dad orders. He cuts the engine and marches inside without waiting to see if we're following.

My mother shoots daggers at me from her eyes. My heart is beating out of my chest. I've never lied to them before. Omitted details, maybe, but flat-out lied? No. I've never had to be punished. I can't even imagine what they're going to do.

"Have a seat on the couch, young lady," Dad says.

I do as I'm told. My parents go into their bedroom to confer before they talk to me. The silent wait is the most excruciating of my life. Going to the principal's office, waiting to get punished, getting rejected from a prestigious program... I have gone my whole life without getting in trouble, and now I can't seem to avoid it. Who am I?

I rock on the couch, clenching every muscle, hoping this is going to end with just a tongue-lashing and being put on punishment for a week. When they come back out, they're a united front, and they are furious. They loom over the couch, and I wish I could sink into the cushions. My dad starts, using a tone of voice he has never directed at me before.

"How long have you been doing this? Don't even try to sell me some made-up crap about you're not doing it or it's only this one time. Radio silence from the grand debater was a clear sign."

I just need to tell the truth. "I don't know. A while."

"Oh, you definitely know. You're not stupid, child," my mom says. "You know. You may not want to admit it, but you know."

"I'm sorry. It started at the end of last year. State, SAT prep, college tours, volunteering… It was just a lot. I was under so much pressure. I needed something to help me balance it all."

"If you were struggling that much, why didn't you talk to me?" The stern demeanor she had melts away. She looks a little hurt, and there's a slight quiver in her voice. "I get that your plate was very full last year. We understand that. Why do you think we gave you the car? But this is not balancing. This is self-medication."

Tears start to leak from my eyes. "I didn't want you to think I couldn't handle it."

"Clearly you cannot, child," Dad says. "Your mom and I have discussed it. You are on punishment, during which time you had better think about what would have happened if you'd been caught by someone other than us."

My mom adds, "I want to make it clear that this is not the end of this conversation, and I will be scheduling an appointment with a therapist so you can get real help."

"I don't know what's gotten into you this year," Dad says. "But it's time you straighten up."

"I'm really sorry." I fight back a loud, ugly cry. "May I be excused?"

My dad nods and waves me away. I run upstairs, slide on my headphones, collapse on my bed, and cry until I'm too exhausted to keep my eyes open anymore.

17

ELEANOR

The downtown campus of Georgia State doesn't look much like the ones pictured in the college brochures that arrived in the mail last year. The urban campus sprawls over a few city blocks, more corporate-looking than collegiate. Other than university logos affixed to the buildings and the number of people walking around with loaded-down backpacks, you wouldn't know you were on the campus of one of the largest colleges in Georgia.

In an alternate universe, Nelly and I would have driven down here together in the Bumblebee. Maybe Three would have come, and I'd have had to squish into the nonexistent back seat of the Bug to accommodate his height. Instead, I'm alone. Somehow, I'm in a weird place with everyone these days. Nelly and I are barely speaking. Three has come over a few times, but he doesn't stay long, and we don't talk the way we used to. It's like the thrill we got at the beginning just from seeing each other, just from talking, has faded.

I zip up my cheer windbreaker against the chilly wind that sweeps between the high-rises. An early cold snap accompanied the last game of the football season. We've only had to wear warms-up during a regular-season football game due to cold one time in my four years of cheering at Franklin. But when the temperature dropped into the forties last Friday, I relented and ordered everyone to layer. We all still shivered our way through the halftime show.

Not pregame, though. We thought the administration would relent once the attention died down. The hallway conversations in school drifted from kneeling to championships when Three record-broke the team's way into the State finals. Everyone moved on, which left a pit in my stomach, though I wasn't able to explain why. We thought that meant the restriction on us would be lifted. There's a tradition during the last game of the season where the underclassmen cheerleaders, along with some of the JV football players, form the tunnel, and the senior cheerleaders get to the lead the football team through it. We thought we'd at least get to participate in that. But Principal Carter didn't back down. Coach Pearce stood in the locker room with a grim look and informed us that there would be no senior tunnel this year, though she'd argued our case to the administration. She'd tried, she promised. But we waited out the last pregame show of our high school cheer careers in the locker room, the tension as thick as the humidity wafting from the leaking shower stall.

No one complained. There were some sighs, some groans, one muttered *of course* from Val. And that was all.

They drowned us out. Defeated us. Things can't end like this.

I find a directory map outside the university MARTA stop and search for the humanities building. According to the university website, Rhonda Matthews, Professor, cochair of the African American Studies department, PhD from the University of California, Berkley 2005, holds office hours on Tuesdays from 4:00 to 7:00 p.m. I'm usually the person with a plan. Between my brain and Nelly's, we always know the right next step. But I can't rely on either of us lately. I need advice from someone who's been in a situation like this. The person I need to talk to is Rhonda.

Her office is on the third floor, down a long hallway lined with identical doors, outside each of which is a professor's nameplate and a corkboard. I glance at the boards as I pass, searching for 324. Some are bare but for printouts announcing people's office hours. One has a single political cartoon pinned to the center—some weird reference to Kant that I don't get, beyond knowing he's a philosopher. One is dedicated to the professor's textbook covers, but they're poorly printed, so the artwork is warped. Quite a few have articles and announcements, and Rhonda's is one of those. Her board overflows with papers tacked on top of one another, fighting for space and attention. I pause, studying them. There are flyers for a voter registration drive, a lecture by a visiting scholar talking about criminal justice reform, and a Monday night meeting of a club called the Leadership Alliance Committee. Articles from a *New York Times* series on race relations are tucked into the edges of the board, quotes from Rhonda herself highlighted in bright yellow. A messy note on one, written in turquoise marker, shouts, GO PROF. MATTHEWS!

A burst of laughter coming from Rhonda's open door startles me, and I jump back, realizing I'd leaned so close my nose almost bumped the corkboard. A guy a few years older than me emerges from the office, slinging on a puffy coat and a backpack as he goes.

"Come back next week, Tariq." Rhonda's voice floats out of the office. "And do *not* bring me another list of tired, uninspired sources for that honors thesis."

Tariq lifts his chin at me. "You're up. She's on fire today, though. Hope you're ready for a sparring match."

I flinch, but he's grinning. There's swagger in his step as he passes me and heads down the hall, reminding me briefly of Three after one of our competitive workouts over the summer. He's got that same I'm-on-top-of-the-world energy, like maybe an academic duel with an on-fire Rhonda is the most fun he's had in a week.

I'm still trying to decide whether I'm up to it when Rhonda calls, "If you're out there, you'd better come on in."

She stands at the desk, head bent over a stack of papers she's shuffling into order. The office reminds me vaguely of Dr. Ratliff's—impersonal industrial furniture and not enough natural light coming through the windows to dispel the gloom. But where his was full of medical books and not much else, Rhonda's bursts with color. Books overflow the shelves and are stacked on the floor. Artwork and blown-up posters of book covers line the walls. There's space enough for a couch and two chairs in addition to the desk and a small glass-topped table.

I hover, waiting for an invitation to enter, for her to look up, but she doesn't, and finally I knock gently on the doorjamb. When she peers over the top of a pair of black-framed reading glasses and catches sight of me, she lets go of the papers.

"Leni," she says. "Well, this is a surprise."

"I don't mean to interrupt," I say, thinking of Tariq and his thesis. I should have asked before coming down here. "This time is probably reserved for your students."

She waves me inside. "You'd be stunned how few students take advantage of these open office hours I dedicate to them. They never come to talk to me about their assignments or the materials we're studying and then get upset when their papers get poor grades." She turns a desk chair to face the couch, settles into it, and points to the spot opposite her. "Sit. It's a surprise, but it's a pleasant one."

I drop my backpack on the floor and take the spot she offers.

"I gather congratulations are due. My nephew and his team made it to the finals for their fourth year in a row."

"He's been playing possessed lately."

"And inking his name deeply into the record books. My brother-in-law thinks it's a hall of fame, Division I performance." She crosses one leg over the other, her blue-and-white printed Toms loafer dangling off her foot. "Do you?"

"Yes." That's an easy question. "I think Three was born for that."

"Hmm," she says. "He's a very driven young man. He works hard."

I nod. But thinking about Three makes my head ache. I'm usually good at dealing with people; it's the number-one soft skill listed on my résumé. That skill seems to have atrophied like the muscles I couldn't use while I was laid up after my falls.

Rhonda reads my mind. "But I don't imagine you've come here today for a chat about Sam's Division I prospects. What can I do for you, Leni?"

"I was wondering if you'd heard what happened to our team after we protested in support of Cody Knight."

"I know some. Why don't you tell me the rest?"

I recap it for her: the fallout, Nelly's suspension, how the administration hasn't let up, and how demoralizing it was. "It feels like they've taken something away from us. I just want to get it back. Or else…or else they've won."

"Who's won, Leni? What battle are you fighting?"

I search for an answer, but none comes. How can I be sitting here feeling so hollow without being able to explain why? "I don't know," I admit. "It's not fair. Nothing that has happened is fair."

The professor smiles, and her eyes soften. Some version of *who promised you life would be fair, kid?* must be going through her mind. I'm grateful she doesn't say it aloud.

She studies me thoughtfully. "Where's your friend Chanel today? I would have thought I'd see the two of you here together. You were quite the tight unit last time I saw you."

My hands twist in my lap, knuckles turning white, a fact I know because I can't stop staring down at them. I feel Rhonda's eyes on the top of my head, burning into my neat part. "She's—we're—" I have a hard time putting words to what's going on with Nelly and me. Admitting aloud that we've barely spoken since the suspension makes it… not real, exactly, because it's already super real, and I know that. But it hurts. "Things are strained at the moment. I think I really screwed up, and I want to make it right."

Rhonda leans forward, resting her elbows on her knees. "Have you asked her what she wants? How she'd like to move forward?"

"I don't know how." A wave a of heat washes over me. I should never have come here.

"I can see that you care a great deal about this, Leni, and that you want to help. I suspect that not knowing what to do is a foreign feeling for you. You remind me of myself not so long ago. You want to make things happen, and you don't have time to wait. I also know that getting somewhere fast doesn't matter if you're heading to the wrong place."

Aaaaaand crash. The wrong place? I shake my head. How will any of this help me figure out what to do about how our school treated us?

"I hate doing nothing, Professor Matthews," I say, hearing the whine in my voice. "There has to be something I can do."

"But doing the *wrong* thing—wouldn't that be a worse mistake? A mistake that could harm the people you're trying to help?"

"How do I know what the wrong thing is?"

She sits back again, and something like annoyance flashes across her face. "Is that why you came here today? So I could tell you what the right thing is?"

I look around the office, my eyes skimming over her desk and her books and her brightly colored art. Anything but her face. I mean, yes. That's exactly why I came here today. But it's clear, suddenly, that that was also the wrong move.

"You know what? I have an idea. Do you go to church?"

My eyebrows knit together. "Uh, I go to synagogue. Sometimes. I'm not very religious."

She waves a hand. "It's more about community, I think. What synagogue do you belong to?"

"Kol Ha'am. It's just north of the city, but—"

"Perfect! Leni, I'm going to give you some homework, all right?" She stands up and fishes around on her desk till she finds her phone, then hands it to me and instructs me to enter my email address. "I'm forwarding you a flyer for a meeting my good friend Rabbi Spinrad leads over at Kol Ha'am."

Rabbi Spinrad? My neighbor is Rhonda's good friend? Somehow, the notion stuns me.

"We've been working together for years," she goes on. "And luckily, they've got some good things starting later this month. Go see Ezra. Go to this meeting." She taps on her phone screen, sending me whatever it is she's so excited about.

"I'm sorry. I really don't understand."

She smiles broadly. "I know. I'm not trying to be mysterious or to discourage you, believe it or not. I'm trying to help. Come see me after you've been to this meeting."

She hasn't resumed her seat. She stands behind her chair and waits, watching me. Her eyes gleam, and her smile seems real. But she's done with this conversation, done with me. I'm not, though. I mean, what did I even get out of this? I'm used to brainstorming problems with Nelly. By the end of a one-hour whiteboarding session in her workroom, we'll have gone through a case of LaCroix, but we'll have a solid plan.

Now? I've got nothing but a forwarded email about a meeting at my own synagogue. I blink, trying to martial my expression into a polite, pleasant one. "Thanks for your time, Professor."

"Good luck, Leni."

I decide to close cheer practices. With football season over and our State qualifier approaching, there is no time for anything but focus. On our new routines. On our timing. On our stunts. I'm still wobbly on the throws, and everyone holds their breath until I come down safely, which is throwing us off. The stress, tension, and disappointment of the last few months haven't helped. We need some space to ourselves.

The administration reluctantly grants Pearce exclusive use of the gym between 5:00 and 6:00 p.m. That works out great, because Paris offers me a ride home with her and Bull and Three, who still work out every day in the weight room even though the football season is over. I haven't seen much of Three lately, so even the short car rides home, his hand touching mine across the back seat of Bull's truck, are a relief. I don't know why I thought things between us would get easier after his practice schedule eased up. It's my busy season now, and by the time Nationals are over—assuming we make it through the qualifier—he'll be deep into track. Time is a luxury neither of us can afford, I guess.

He's waiting for me on Wednesday, pacing just outside the gym door, which is odd, because normally Paris and I have to drag him and Bull out of the weight room.

"Did you go see my aunt?" he demands as soon as I emerge from the gym. His light skin is flushed, and sweat is beaded along his brow.

I stop short. The team is still milling around, some filtering down the walkway toward the parking lot, others straggling behind me. But every single one of them is in earshot.

I wonder whether Rhonda told him or whether she told her sister, who told him. God, I hope it wasn't Three's mom. She would have made it sound like the worst thing in the world.

There's no point in lying. "Yes."

"Leni," he says, sounding tired, "I asked you not to do that."

I straighten up. It's a little difficult with the weight of

everyone's eyes on me. The air around us sizzles. "I deserve a little more respect than that. It wasn't about you. Your name barely even came up."

"But I heard *your* name from my mother. I don't need to be hearing from her about what you're getting up to with my aunt, okay? You're making things worse."

"Is this you talking, Three, or your dad?"

His nostrils flare. "You know what? I think it's best we both walk away right now."

He starts to do that, but I follow. "You're allowed to have your own opinions, you know." I shouldn't be throwing this at him. I know it's too much. But I can't seem to turn down my internal temperature.

He swings around, his gym bag banging against him. He clenches the strap tightly with both hands. "Well, my opinion is that I don't need no unnecessary distractions."

"Are you saying *I'm* a distraction?" It's gotten hotter in the hallway, and I'm having a hard time focusing on anything other than that.

"Nah, Leni. You're not even that."

A collective gasp shrieks in my ears. Everyone who has stuck around to watch—the team, whoever Three was working out with—sucks all the oxygen out of the air at once, and I get dizzy. Three's halfway to the exit, practically racing out. He slams a hand against a locker as he passes, and the bang echoes down the hall.

I stand there, my ears ringing loud enough to drown out the voices around me until a heavy hand rests on my back. I blink Bull's bulky chest into focus. His arm is outstretched between us, and he's bent a bit so he can look into my eyes.

"You cool, Leni?"

I nod. Then shake my head. Then nod again. "Did he just break up with me? Over this?"

"How's he gonna break up with someone he was never really with?"

"Bull!" Paris smacks his arm.

She's beside him, the two of them blocking out the rest of the hallway. Maybe they're shielding me. I breathe a little deeper.

"I'm not trying to be harsh," Bull says out of the corner of his mouth, aiming the words at Paris, "but someone's gotta be honest with her, or she's gonna go and do this same thing with a third dude."

"She don't need your TED Talk about how girls jump levels," Paris argues. "Not right now."

"That's exactly what she needs," he says. He sets his other hand on my other shoulder and claims my attention. "Look, Leni. You're acting like a girlfriend when you're not. You're too much too fast, and he just ain't there with you."

A third time? Bull's words sink into my soul. He means Roman. There's a sob building in my chest. I don't want to let it out here. He's wrong. It's different with Three.

Paris gives Bull a shove, releasing me from his grip but also exposing me to the rest of the crowd, which, of course, has stuck around to witness the drama. The show's still going on. "Bull, get out of here. Me and Leni will get a ride with Val."

He hesitates. "Don't be mad, Leni. I'm just trying to protect you."

"I'm not mad," I say too loud. It's better than a whisper. "I'm fine."

I'm not fine.

The world sounds hollow for the next few days. The teachers' lectures are muffled, as though they're in the next room. Practices pass, and I barely remember them. I end each night with four or five missed phone calls, members of the team calling to check on me or mine for gossip. I don't remember hearing my phone ring. I don't call them back.

Since the concussion, I've slipped from anger to sadness easily, and when I sink into it, it's hard to climb out. I have wanted so badly to believe all the effects from the falls were in the past, but they're not. My parents and the doctors all keep saying there are pieces of this that I will have to manage forever. This is the new me.

And the new me doesn't know what to do. Is Three

right? His aunt seemed like the person to talk to. It never occurred to me that she'd tell his mom I'd been to see her.

Okay, that's not actually true. I just didn't consider how *he'd* feel about it. I'm sorry for that. I burn to text him—my phone finds its way into my hands a hundred times—but I don't know what I'd write. Nelly's voice in my head says that if I don't know what to say, I shouldn't advertise it to the world.

I miss her.

I've never felt so lost.

Maybe it's that aimless feeling that pulls me in the direction of Rhonda's homework, though I didn't plan to go to the meeting she emailed me about. Mom hands over her car keys, eyebrows running up her forehead when I announce that I'm going to the synagogue. Her default mode these days is watching me closely but silently. My mother is not the silent type. She's the pepper-you-with-questions type. *What are you looking forward to this school year? Tell me one thing you learned today. How did you improve between that last project and this one?* She used to log in to the school portal daily to "check my progress." The only conversations that ever came out of that, though, were about why my grades weren't higher and whether I was spending too much time at practice. She never wanted to talk about the progress I was making on my stunts and tumbling. Shocker. Around eighth grade, the topics of

PSATs, SATs, reach schools, safety schools, and application deadlines began to dominate her Q&A sessions.

She eased up last year after the concussions, her questions less demanding, her tone gentler...until recently, when the earliest of early acceptances rolled in. When her friends started posting pics of their kids in college gear and applying stickers to their cars that said GEORGIA MOM or whatever. When it became clear *she* wasn't going to get to post a picture like that of her own any time soon. Then she went completely silent.

I can't believe I'm saying this, but her silence is worse than the interrogations. Because I know it's hiding the exact same anxiety that wakes *me* up twice a night.

It doesn't help to think about that. College worries are too big to hold in my mind. What I can focus on is this meeting with Rabbi Spinrad.

The synagogue receptionist directs me the library. In the open space in the center, the tables have been arranged in a rough U shape. I'm a bit late. The seats at the table are full, and Rabbi Spinrad is already speaking. I sneak in and snag a chair outside of the U, sinking down and pretending to myself that the lateness was an accident, that I'd be sitting front and center if it didn't mean interrupting the meeting and making a spectacle of myself.

I observe the assembled group. I don't know anyone, which is probably not all that odd, considering how little time I've spent here lately. And considering everyone in the room is at least a decade older than me. *At least.* Quite a few look old enough to be my grandparents. I do recognize the women coleading the meeting—Gisela Katz Rodriguez. Her son, David, who was in my bar/bat mitzvah class, was hands down the best at chanting Torah.

"We're in final preparation mode for the expungement clinic," Gisela is saying. "We've had excellent participation in the training sessions. I'm going to hand my imaginary microphone over to the director of outreach for our partner organization, Clean Records Georgia. For those of you who haven't met her yet, this is our partner and friend, Letitia Sadler."

The Black woman sitting beside Gisela smiles. "Thank you all for having me. This has been an enormous effort over the course of the last year—CRG has been so grateful for the strong working relationship we've forged with this group and the other community partners necessary to hold a record restriction clinic. I've been finalizing preparations with the district attorney's office, the solicitor general's office, and the county commissioner. With your volunteers staffing the event, in one day, the streamlined process we've developed will help clear records of arrests, minor charges, pretrial diversion program participation, and more. We're expecting hundreds of people, all of whom will leave this building with improved prospects for employment and securing housing and with fewer collateral consequences for being a formerly incarcerated person."

Her speech captivates me, both the subject and her passion for it. When the meeting moves on to logistical matters for the day of the clinic, I Google her organization and read about how they're one of the few nonprofits working on criminal record restriction in the state. This sounds like something my mother would be into. I wonder if it's too late for her to participate.

Rabbi Spinrad picks up once Ms. Sadler has concluded. "All right, team. I know we've been working hard on the clinic, and I don't want to draw energy away from that, but we had three goals this year. One, partnering with CRG on this clinic; two, running at least two voter registration drives; and three, expanding the membership of this social justice group to include our youth. As you know, Intown Baptist, which our friend and mentor Professor Rhonda Matthews attends, has a youth group focused on social justice, and they've been asking if we might like to partner with them."

Gisela clears her throat. "Ezra, I think I see the solution to that problem sitting in the back of this room right now."

My spine goes stiff. Oh no—I was supposed to be here incognito. I'm just listening. I shake my head, eyes wide. But she laughs.

"I won't put you on the spot, but I'm glad to see you here. And I'm going to tell David you came. I've been trying to get him to attend a meeting for months, but he says this is a group for old people. I can't wait to prove him wrong."

A tense, embarrassed smile pastes itself on my mouth, because that's not far off from what I was thinking.

"Leni, we are very glad to have you join us," Rabbi Spinrad says.

Join them? That's…interesting. What would that involve? I open my mouth to ask, but he's moved on. They're talking about some upcoming college fair and their work with Intown and other things, but I've lost the thread. Although I'm intrigued by the work this group is doing, I can't help but wonder why Rhonda sent me here. None of this has anything to do with our team expressing how we feel about a social issue and being unfairly punished for it. I think of Nelly, and my stomach twists.

I try to sneak out as soon as the meeting breaks up, but the rabbi catches me. He asks me to wait for a few minutes while he says goodbye to the others. It takes him almost half an hour because everyone has something particular to discuss with him—whether the group needs more members, whether the Purim carnival needs more volunteers, whether he can give a talk at their office/school/neighborhood association about the work the synagogue's been doing.

"Come on," he says when everyone else has departed at last. "I'll walk you to your car."

Hands in the pockets of his slacks, he wanders slowly

beside me through the quiet building toward the parking garage. The synagogue is weird at this time of night—quiet, still. All the evening education groups have concluded by now, and it's just the staff finishing up and closing down. It's kinda creepy.

"I am glad you came," Rabbi Spinrad says.

I glance over and realize he might be glad, but he's not surprised. "You knew I'd be here?"

"I had a heads-up, you might say." He smiles. "I've known Rhonda for years. She's an impressive advocate in the community. You couldn't ask for a better mentor as you get started in this work."

"She's not my mentor." I recall how desperately Three wanted me to stay away from her. I know we're not together; I guess we never really were. But I'm positive he doesn't want me chasing after his aunt now. "And the thing is, I don't really know why she sent me here."

He pauses beside a display honoring the synagogue's history and studies me. "Don't you?"

"No. I mean, I went to see her a couple of weeks ago. To talk to her about the administration at school. About how they treated us."

"You weren't celebrated as heroes by the principal, huh? Were you surprised by that?"

"No, but I am surprised by how far they took it. They threw us off the field."

"And that's not what you expected?"

My mother's too-full key ring feels like a twenty-pound weight in my hands. "Nothing happened. That's the problem. We created all this momentum. Other clubs and groups at school joined us. Then the administration shut down everything we were trying to do, and it all faded quietly away."

"Ah," he says in his wise-rabbi voice. "You know one thing our friend Rhonda taught me? Moments are not movements."

I shake my head. "I'm not good with metaphors."

"Moments attract a lot of attention, and they are important. They can kick-start things. But the real work is behind the scenes. It's not always social media–worthy."

"That's not why we did it," I say.

He quirks an eyebrow and hits the elevator button. "I'm glad to hear that. You should be proud of what happened and how you handled it as a squad. But now, I think it's time to focus on what's next for all of you. David is interested in doing a voter registration table at the Intown Church college fair, but it's a big job for one person, and he's got soccer too. Maybe think about cochairing with him."

"A voter registration table?" I laugh. "I'm not even old enough to vote."

"No, but I bet you're old enough to register. You should start with yourself."

He walks a few steps, searching the framed pictures hanging on the wall and stopping before one of the most famous and iconic images. It's a photo of the head rabbi from the sixties in a civil rights march, walking in a group of men all wearing light-colored trench coats and ties, fedoras on their heads. The rabbi stands in the second or third row, carrying a sign that's cut off at the top of the picture. "You know the story of this image, right?"

I nod. We all know how our rabbi joined in the movement in the sixties, even getting arrested with a group of clergy that protested segregation at the state capital.

"Why do you think we have this picture on the wall?"

"To celebrate our contribution to the movement," I say.

"Hmmm," he says. His wise-rabbi voice is back, telling me my answer was wrong. "Our contribution? Were we at that march?"

I frown. This congregation celebrates that moment so much. Is he telling me we shouldn't?

"We don't get to claim ownership of their work. It's not about *our* contribution. To me, it's a reminder that the work isn't done. Living up to a legacy doesn't mean celebrating it. It means we pick up the baton and keep running the race. It also means we need to check ourselves and our assumptions about how far we've come, or haven't. We have antiracism work to do here. There are Black members of this community who are subjected to microaggressions within these walls, who are made to feel like outsiders. How can we go about tikkun olam when that's how we're treating our own members? The prior generation's participation doesn't absolve us of our responsibility to keep doing the work, internally and in the broader community."

His words are a bit of an awakening—and honestly, I know that's kind of unacceptable. But I'm not sure where to go from here. "So, that's what you think is the right next step for me? Doing voter registration stuff?"

"I can't answer that for you, Leni. It's up to you to decide. But the fact that you're here tells me you're seeking to do better. Don't give yourself a pass. Your good intentions are not enough."

I think of the way I tried to persuade everyone to do a walkout or a protest in school. The way I *pushed*. I remember how many organizations Letitia said are participating in the record restriction project. I think for so long that we miss the elevator and the doors close again. "Rabbi Spinrad, can I ask you something? Whose idea was that expungement clinic?"

He grins. "Gisela is a lawyer. She came across the CRG at a pro bono fair her firm hosted and wanted to get involved, so she asked what kind of support they were looking for. They'd been trying to hold a record restriction clinic for a while, and Gisela came to the social justice committee and asked if it was something we'd support.

Then the committee started meeting with the CRG to see what they needed that we could help provide. They needed a location, and they needed volunteers. So that's what we're providing."

I think of how Rhonda asked me how the rest of the squad was, how Nelly was. I think of Three's frustration when I talked about walkouts. I think of how I haven't asked either of them what's going on in their heads.

And suddenly, I realize I have a lot more thinking to do.

18

CHANEL

There's a tap on my door. "Who is it?"

The door cracks open. Alana sticks her head inside. "I'm here to see prisoner 6975967456."

We both laugh. "Does the warden know you're here? My visiting hours have been severely restricted."

"She knows. I've heard there's a pardon coming down today."

"That's what I'm told too."

She comes in and plops onto my bed. Alana's far more petite than me, and she's recently cut her hair in an extremely neat bob. She's still dressed in her college clothes, which make her look like an eighties country club member. Today's shirt is cashmere and has faux pearl button detail. "How are you doing, kiddo?"

I'm feeling better now that my sister and I are together. "Grateful to see you. How long are you back for?" Alana usually comes home for a week at Thanksgiving, but I know this has been an unusually busy year for her.

"Only a few days. I have an early final, so I need the peace and quiet of my apartment. You know Dad is on my case about grad school applications. I won't get any studying done with him hovering and Mom cross-referencing her sorors to find every alumni networking event in a fifty-mile radius!"

The best part about Alana is having someone who understands what I normally experience. But honestly, her words are also hard to hear right now. We've been so busy fixing my unexpected disciplinary problems, we haven't been able to focus on my college applications. I would really like to get back to a family norm that includes me being harassed about plans instead of suspension.

Luckily, the removal of the suspension from my permanent record finally came through. Ms. Murphy has submitted my transcripts and her recommendations to my top choices, Penn and Cornell. After everything that's happened, she also suggested some safety schools, so we added Purdue, Carnegie Mellon, Northeastern, Kentucky, and UNC-Chapel Hill. I know they don't have the best business schools, but I have to admit she may be right. Smart people put safety nets in place.

I can't help but notice the way my parents talk to Alana about grad school like it's a guarantee is the opposite of how they talk to me about top-tier colleges like they're an aspiration, like despite my high hopes, they think I'm just shooting my shot to see where it lands. I am so happy for her, and I don't begrudge her the excitement, even if I am disappointed things aren't happening for me the way I expected them to.

"How's the pressure from Dad been?" Alana asks. "Let me know if you need some tricks I've learned to manage him."

"He's icing me out. It's almost like he's lost faith in me." In some ways, I've lost faith in me too.

"Impossible. No one could lose faith in the wonder kid."

"That's you," I say. "You're the flawless one."

"I might be good at following a path consistently. No one worries about whether I'm going to have a certain level of success. But you're going to change the world, baby sister."

I tear up and lean my head on Alana's shoulder. I didn't realize it, but I've needed this. I've needed Alana. It's been a long time since I've been reminded how people used to view me.

She pushes my hair back. "If you take anything from me, take this: get back to planning. The mistake wasn't what you did. It was going about it carelessly. Haven't you noticed that the first time you decided to do something without a plan, it bit you in the butt?"

"My head is just so clouded. I don't even know where to start."

"Are you talking about this with your therapist?"

"Yes, and it's helping me process my feelings."

"Well, what about the others who are going through this? Like Leni?"

Hearing Leni's name is a gut punch. "It's really hard to talk to her right now. I'm the only one suffering any real consequences here, and Leni's just living her little golden life, with her boyfriend and her captaincy. It feels like we're breaking up."

"Eventually, I hope you revisit your understanding of what's going on with her, but for now, let's just focus on you." She hands me a tissue from the AKA-decorated tissue box I borrowed from my mom with no intention of returning it. "Listen. Have you thought about a peer support group? Sometimes it's easier to talk to people who are in the same place in life as you."

"My therapist recommended one. But I don't know."

"You know, I go to one frequently, through the student mental health clinic."

It surprises me to hear that. Alana always seems so sure of herself.

"Freshman year, I had an anxiety attack. I realized I'd been having them for a while, but I didn't know what they were. My roommate brought me to the clinic on campus, and they hooked me up with a peer group. It was a relief not to have to handle the pressure all alone anymore and to have accountability to share the load."

"Why didn't you tell me about this?" I ask.

"You have a Superwoman complex about me, Nelly. That's a lot to live up to. I'm constantly afraid of letting you down and setting the wrong example."

"You are? Meanwhile, I'm only ever trying to keep up with you."

We sit there side by side on my bed for a moment.

"So the peer group really helps you?"

"It does," she says.

Maybe I will give it a try.

If this room weren't in a medical building, you might mistake it for the offices of a tech start-up; it has beanbag chairs, a foosball table, and a cereal bar in the corner with a huge selection of sugary cereals I don't allow myself to eat. I head straight for my favorite purple fleece throw and wrap myself up before joining the circle of my peers. Everyone's become used to seeing me swaddled in this blanket during these therapy sessions. Opening up took a while, but I had no choice but to let my guard down once I watched the others being so vulnerable. It seemed to be freeing for them. I'm still working on being that free. I have certain days when sharing is a struggle, but I am proud of how far I've come. For example, today, when the counselor says we're going to talk about techniques for resolving past hurts, I don't escape within myself. I participate.

Opal goes first. "I'm still processing my breakup with Chase. I look at our text chain every day, trying to read between the lines and see where I lost him, see where I could have done something different."

"Opal," I say. "Be kinder to yourself. I went through something similar—not a romantic breakup, but I'm no longer speaking to my best friend. The desire to continue to communicate with her doesn't just turn off like a faucet."

"What did you do about it?"

"I'm still working on it, honestly."

Our group leader, Mariah, who sits in the circle with us, leans forward on her beanbag. "Have you all tried any other forms of expression? Art? Writing? How about journaling?"

Another group member says, "I kinda like journaling. I've been doing it for three months. It's different from school writing. I like that there are no rules. And it helps me not have knee-jerk reactions anymore."

Mariah nods. "It's like a way to think feelings through in advance."

It seems like it would be much easier to have hard conversations if I had my talking points in place. Just like I opened myself up to this group, maybe I should give journaling a try. I used to come into every situation with an agenda, but group is teaching me to listen and then react. I'm discovering that I do genuinely want to help people. I just have to take my personal wants out of the equation and do what's best for them. Now I need to figure out how best to do that and how to balance it all. I know who to go see to help me finalize my thoughts too.

I'm sitting on the tank of the toilet, using a toilet seat cover to block a few germs, when the door slowly creaks open. My heart beats a little harder. I don't know why I'm so nervous. It's just a conversation. I remind myself that I'm not being judged here.

"I don't detect the distinct smell of air freshener this time."

We both let out a little giggle. My hands unclench as the laughter helps me relax. The old me never would have laughed at Marisol's joke about our first meeting. But my emerging friendship with her is a soft place to land, even when I'm not at my best.

"I may have retired that habit," I say, exiting the stall. It feels good to say so out loud. Outside of group, there's no one else I can talk to like this. Spending less time with Leni has alerted me to how few friends I have.

"Found another outlet?"

"Yep. I've been going to therapy. Your messages have helped as well." Marisol smiles with pride.

Over the past few months, we've been texting constantly, but we've both been so busy that even finding this moment to meet took some major schedule manipulation.

In the meantime, we've become each other's voices of reason and each other's support systems during the stress of college acceptance season. Her situation isn't exactly the same as mine, because she doesn't have a disciplinary record, but the competition level at the schools where she's applying is extreme. I know she checks her email ten times an hour, hoping she'll hear something from MIT.

"How was date night?" I ask. She and Londie have been trying to maximize their time together before we all head off to the next part of our lives.

"For real? It was heavy." Marisol picks a stray piece of lint off her dark denim cutoffs. Today she's paired them with a pair of beige Yeezys and a beige hoodie with the Mercury space shuttle logo, which I'm pretty sure she brought back from her internship with NASA last summer. "We're still trying to figure out if we're going to do the long-distance thing."

No matter where Marisol ends up, Londie won't be there. She signed a commitment letter with Purdue way back in February.

Low-key, I think it's better if they don't try to make

it work. Marisol doesn't need the distraction with such a difficult program ahead of her. Then again, she's not the type to let a relationship be her downfall. And it's not my decision; it's hers. "Either way," I tell her, "I know you'll find your happiness."

"So, what's up, buttercup? Why the secret hangout?"

"I wanted to get your advice." She has never been anything short of real with me. One of the things we've been going over in group is authenticity in our intentions. I have an idea about where I'm headed again, but I couldn't think of anyone more true to the core than Marisol. She will call me out if I'm swinging in a selfish direction.

"Shoot."

"I want to do more community work, but I need to find something that's authentic to me."

"Looking to pad your community service before final admissions decisions are made?" There it is—that signature Marisol-brand honesty I knew was coming. I wish I could throw my words into the trash like scratch paper and start all over.

"No. I want something I can connect to. One of the things Leni has always had right is how she connects with people on a personal level. Even though the cheer team is disappointed in Leni right now, I feel like if they ran into her in a mall in twenty years, they'd still want to get coffee with her and catch up. I'm just trying to foster more of that in my own life."

Marisol scrunches her face. That came out way more attention-seeking than I intended.

"Okay, so you've told me what Leni is good at. What do you bring to the table?"

There was a time when I would have answered that question with speed and confidence. It's not that I don't know what I bring to the table; it's more like I want to make sure I'm bringing the *right* things.

"I'm very organized. I'm a big-picture person. I can lay out a successful plan and see it through."

"Then do that," she says. "Listen, don't devalue the importance of who you are. Community organizing is nothing without the organizing part. You're a stabilizer. That's super important."

Marisol leans in for a side hug and leaves. I have a little time before my next period, so I sit. She's given me a lot to think about. Dealing with the fallout from our protest became as consuming as the college admissions process. It took over my life. I wonder now if that was my own fault. The number of web searches I did about disciplinary records and their effect on college applications was impossible to count. And that pressure led me to being stoned for nearly two months. I easily could have used that time to figure out a way to move from protest to action. Instead, I created an escape. No lie, I still sometimes think about that escape, but I'm trying to recalibrate, and I'm ready to move toward action with a functional plan in place.

Tonight, the squad goes out to celebrate our win at State. Before we took the stage, Coach gave us an Oscar-worthy speech about her last conversation with the administration, filled with highs and lows. She said we'd be allowed onto the court for pregame during the basketball season, but only if we did not kneel.

She allowed us to make our own decision, and it was Paris who said it. "Then we don't need to go out."

Val pumped his fist. "We'd rather stay in the locker room."

There was a general consensus, and then we went out and slayed our State routine.

We didn't do anything wrong. We all stand by that.

19

ELEANOR

We're on a football field, which should feel like home.

But this one doesn't. This is the centerpiece of Disney's All-Star Sports Resort. Instead of bleachers, it's surrounded by blocks of hotel rooms. Two giant, two-hundred-foot-tall football helmets lead the way into the stairwells. There are no guys in shoulder pads on this field, either. Instead, every square inch is crowded with cheer teams, wearing school warm-ups in every color you can imagine and, of course, matching bows.

Tomorrow, the national championship semifinals begin at the ESPN Wide World of Sports Complex. We arrived and checked in yesterday, and everything has felt like total chaos since. Tens of thousands of cheerleaders and coaches and families fill this space. The athletes are simultaneously practicing and trying to scope out the competition without looking like that's what we're doing.

"Check them out," Val hisses as we walk down the field, searching for an open area to practice. I follow his gaze to a team dressed all in black. The Florida sun sparkles on the metallic panther logos on their shirts and shorts—on the front of the leg for the guys and on one ass cheek for the girls. I'd roll my eyes, except I'm too busy goggling over the precision of their pop-ups. Not one wobble. Not a hand out of place.

I should say something confident back. I should encourage him, tell him we're just as good but that we need to keep our eyes on our own paper. I don't manage to get out the words before Coach Pearce calls back to us to hustle.

"Bags over here," she yells. "Circle up!"

We drop our things in a pile and gather around her. She wears dark red lipstick, made up even out here in the blazing heat on a warm-up day. We all are too. No one looks at a bedraggled team like they might be something to worry about, even if it is just a practice day. You can't slack on your mental game.

"I know there's a lot of distraction," Coach says, shouting to be heard over the chanting. "That's why we're here on this field right now. Y'all need to get accustomed to the chaos. You'll be alone on that performance stage, but you'll still be in a room full of people. It won't be like cheering at a home game. It won't feel like a friendly crowd. It'll feel like they're all judging you, because they will be. It's State to the power of ten. The way to stay strong is to look to each other—not the crowd, not your families, not even me. Your pillars are your teammates."

Normally, someone would give a *woo-hoo* to that kind of speech. Today, we're all silent, dinner plate–sized eyes sliding from Coach to the teams around us. I know I need to speak up.

"I'm proud to be a part of this team." My voice is clear and loud. They turn to me. I know that pieces of the binding that used to hold us together are torn, and nothing I say today can stitch them back together perfectly. "We deserve to be here. We're resilient. No matter what happens, it's not just about today. It's about our legacy. We've earned this."

I probably should've saved this speech for tomorrow, when we're waiting in the wings for our turn on the mat. But this feels like the right moment. I look at Nelly the whole time I'm talking. I've made so many mistakes. I could spend all day every day wishing for a do-over, wishing so hard that I become trapped in it. But that would only make me freeze up and prevent me from doing better now.

"Chanel is the architect of our routine," I say. "I want to acknowledge that we never would have made it here without her leadership. If she'll take them, I'd like to hand the reins to her."

Her face is serious for three long beats, and I feel as if I've parachuted out of an airplane. Will she accept this as the apology I mean it to be? Forever passes before she smiles and steps forward. "Gladly. We know this routine. Today is about polishing it. We just need to be clean, crisp, and on-target with our timing. Let's go."

We sail through semifinals with a high score, but the day of the finals, nerves set in. Yesterday doesn't mean anything. Every day is a new performance, and I'm intimidated. The teams at the tops of their panel are near perfect, which is what we need to be if we want to win. We're all feeling the pressure. I see it in the frowns of my teammates, in the way their eyes dart around, assessing the competition. They clutch their gym bags and stick close to one another, moving as an inseparable block lest the crowd dissolve us.

Not Paris, though. She's as chill as ever, dancing through the crowds in the sports complex to an upbeat tempo that's playing in her head. Every few steps, she stops to Snapchat or text Bull one of the hundreds of pictures she's been sending him since our bus pulled out of the school parking lot back in Atlanta. When he calls on FaceTime, she answers, even though we're still in the middle of the crowd. She waves us over, and we huddle around her phone while Bull and a couple of the guys from the offensive line perform one of our sideline cheers. They're awful—no precision, sloppy stunts, and mismatched pom-poms. But they also wear enormous grins, shouting at top volume to be heard over the background noise. Their hype crackles over the phone line and sends a jolt of energy into me. I smile for the first time today. All of us do.

The world flies by in fast-forward—Coach's pep talk, makeup check, warm-ups, final tumbling practice. Before I have a chance to process my nerves, we're standing on the mat in front of a Cinderella's castle background and the straight-backed competition spotters. A huge room filled with screaming people sprawls before us. As I run out and set down the pom-poms and signs we need for our routine, I gaze past the camera crew directly in front of the stage to the faces of the parents, friends, and families packed in behind them. I spy Coach and our parent chaperones cheering with their arms over their heads, and it does nothing to settle the buzzing in my legs—especially once I spot my own parents waving frantically. It's the first major competition they've ever traveled to, and my grin almost bursts off my face at the sight of them. I whirl around to take my place, and as I see the team in perfect formation, my pulse steadies. My head doesn't twinge. I've left most of the worst effects of the concussions behind me. I'm ready. *We're* ready.

Nelly lifts me into the air for that first basket toss, and it's crisp and confident.

I'm flying again.

When our routine ends, I'm shaking from exertion, but

also excitement. I slide down from the last lift, straight into Nelly's hug. Her arms are so tight around me. I clutch her, too, and we're jumping and screaming. The others go wild around me. From the corner of my eye, I see our alternates on the sidelines, holding each other back so no one runs onto the mat to surround us. It's a point deduction if they do. But I know why they want to.

We were perfect.

The judges will find deductions to take. Maybe a tiny timing blip here and there, maybe a few claps out of sync. Anything to keep from handing us a perfect score sheet. But I don't need that. I already know how we did. Looking around, I can tell we all feel it.

Later that afternoon, it's official. Franklin is named the national champion of the Small Varsity Coed competition. We receive medals and white satin national champion bomber jackets. The temperature is in the seventies—way too hot for a jacket of any kind—but no one takes them off for the rest of the day. In fact, we all show up for the bus ride home still wearing them, and I have a feeling we'll all wear them right through the warm Georgia spring.

———

Our win merits a mention on the morning announcements that week and a single paragraph in the school paper, not even a headline. The team smiles weakly when friends and teachers congratulate us in the hallways. We accept the high fives directed our way, but I can tell we all ache inside, thinking of the schoolwide, half-day pep rally the football team received when they won. It was practically a carnival. The principal doesn't even show up to deliver his congratulations in person. He sends Coach Pearce with a message that she reads from her phone.

"It's bullshit," Bull says the Friday after our triumph. A few of us stand in the front hallway before the floor-to-ceiling display case of trophies. Ours is in there, shiny and new, the first National High School Cheerleading Championship Franklin has ever won.

Nelly shakes her head. "What did you expect? The administration made its feelings clear back in the fall. We're persona non grata at this school. I don't even know if the team will get a clean slate next year."

"Well, you're not persona non anything to me," he declares, jumping up on one of the benches in the hall. "Shemar! DeWayne! Tristan! Cole! Get over here."

"Bull, you're wild." Paris grabs his backpack and tugs, but she's laughing. "What're you up to?"

"If they won't throw you the celebration of the century, I will." He raises his voice and shouts to the audience around him, "Did y'all know these badass women right here won their own national championship?"

Second lunch is about over, and people have begun

to spill out of the cafeteria. They can't help but gather to see the spectacle. The guys Bull called, whom I recognize from the offensive line, trot over, dragging a few others with them. Nervously, I glance toward the administrative offices. The secretaries have stood up behind the desk to see what's going on. A few vice principals and the nurse file out to watch. I cross my fingers that the principal isn't around.

"They've cheered on every team during every game, and I think it's time they get to hear us doing a little cheering for them!"

The guys from the team groan and shove each other. Then they shove Bull right off that bench. But they're all smiling, and a grin is creeping across my face too. I sneak a peek at Nelly, and she's shaking her head, arms crossed over her chest. She can't keep the amusement from her face as Bull lines the guys up and they launch into the cheer they did for us over FaceTime. It's a well-known one from Friday night games, and by the time they're on the second round of the chant, the crowd has joined in.

We're surrounded by voices shouting for us, and suddenly, bittersweet tears well in my eyes. It's not the pep rally I'd been dreaming of, with a speech by the principal and my parents in the crowd. But not one of these students is here because they have to be or because they want a free period. Maybe some are here just to see the spectacle, but the energy in the room, the way the cheer swells as Bull and the guys name everyone on the team, tell me that many—maybe even most—are here for us. For a few moments at the end of a lunch period, that really feels like something.

I know from IG that Three is traveling, and I can't help but torture myself by wondering if he would've shown up if he were in town. Would he be chanting my name with the rest of the guys? If I'm truthful, I know he wouldn't, and that stings more than I want to admit.

When the bell rings and the reverberating chants fade, Bull takes his backpack, which Paris has been holding, and grabs her in his trademark bear hug.

"You're too much," she says.

"I think I'm just enough," he replies. "I also think I'm throwing y'all a party tonight. My house, eight o'clock. Spread the word."

———

Most of the football and cheer teams plus a ton of our other friends show up at Bull's house. His parents have filled tubs with ice and sodas, and there are trays of Publix subs and chicken nuggets spread around the basement. Bull tunes the TV to ESPN College, which is recapping National Signing Day. A clean-cut, handsome anchorman babbles about the various big signings, a montage of athletes signing papers and putting on the hats of their newly committed schools flashes across the screen. An endless stream of people achieving their dreams. The sight of them reminds me of my empty inbox—the one I created specially to email college cheer programs. No invitations to spring tryouts have arrived. In fact, most of my introductory emails to coaches have gone unanswered. And, thanks to my unremarkable grades, I've already been waitlisted at two schools.

I'll never have the celebratory day the players signing commitment letters are having. I'm not even sure I'll still be cheering in the fall. At the thought that maybe my career is just...done, I ache. How will I fill all the time I planned to spend at practice and games? Who will my friends be if I don't have a team?

And then, suddenly, Three's face lights up the screen.

We haven't spoken since that day in the hallway after practice. The team has been on alert ever since, cordoning us off from each other. Maneuvering me to sit on the opposite side of the lunchroom. Warning me if he'd be at some party I wanted to go to. Shutting down gossip. When I realized that's what they were up to, I was stunned. They've never circled around me like that before. The pressure of this year has turned us into genuine friends where literally hundreds of hours of practice, performing, and competing together failed. They've done their best to shield me, but it's not like they can erase him from the planet.

I see him around school. Football is over, and spring

track hasn't started, so technically, it's his off-season. But Three doesn't take time off. He's been in the weight room. I thought about turning up at the workout oval at the park, orchestrating a "coincidental" meeting. I've managed to avoid stooping to that level, though only barely. But I'm not even trying to avoid hearing gossip about him. It feels like the entire country has been speculating about where he's going to sign. His dad's all over social media, generating as much hype as there is for a presidential election. I can't imagine what he'll be like four years from now on NFL Draft Day. If Lamont doesn't go into sports PR after this, he's missing his calling, I swear.

Everyone in Bull's basement screams when they see Three on the screen. The party pauses. The flow of people pulls me along in its wake to the edge of the crowd gathered around the TV, which displays an image of our QB at a table draped with a bright orange cloth. Behind him, there's a matching orange background studded with paw prints. He wears a neat black suit with a carefully knotted lavender tie and a pocket square. His hair is freshly cut, a low fade with shorter twists than he usually wears. That smile of his, the one that still draws an answering smile out of me, seems to stretch from one edge of the screen to the other. His father sits on one side of him, a hand on Three's shoulder, and on his other sits an older white man I don't recognize. They're both angled toward Three. The shot is framed with him in the exact middle. He's the literal and figurative center of attention.

He looks as comfortable as he would on his sofa. He belongs there.

"Alan, would you say this was your most anticipated signing?" one anchor says, turning to his cohost, while the screen splits to a shot of Three settling a Clemson hat on his head.

"I believe I would, Pete. Sam Walters—or maybe I should say his father, Lamont, a controversial figure in his own right—kept us guessing until this morning. They took some surprise meetings with Oregon and even Georgia, which many thought was a real possibility, given that he'd be a hometown favorite. But in the end, why wouldn't the number-one prospect go with the top-ranked team?"

Pete nods and puts on a concerned face. "This young record-holding quarterback became embroiled in a bit of controversy earlier this year that some thought might have an impact on this day."

The room erupts in boos. Bull shushes them frantically.

"We caught up with Cody Knight, who spoke out in support of Walters just days ago."

A voiceover plays, the key quote appearing on the screen. "I'm proud of this fine young athlete for his conviction as well as his talent. I can say, having been where he is, that he's the product of an excellent high school football program that has prepared him to be a top-notch addition to any college team. I have confidence that a coach will see him for the leader he is and understand the passion he will bring to everything he does, especially the game. I look forward to the day I face off against Sam Walters across an offensive line."

"Quite an endorsement from Cody Knight," Alan says.

"Hard to argue with Knight, a subject of controversy himself, who answered his critics with his best pro season yet."

"You said it, Pete. You think he'll still be in the league when Walters makes his start?"

Pete laughs, not the usual disingenuous laugh of a TV news anchor. It's the laugh of someone who's been caught off guard. "I think you should never count Cody Knight out of anything, Alan. Not one thing."

The news moves on. The party does, too, as I sink into a corner of the couch, feeling a combination of things I don't have words to describe. Relief for Three that he gets to realize his dreams might be strongest, but it's paired with a heavy stab of jealousy. His next step is set. I'm still so very adrift. But he's worked hard for this his whole life, and I know how that feels. A wave of excitement washes away my self-centered dread. I imagine myself sitting in his seat at that table, or the cheerleading equivalent. I imagine myself heading off to Kentucky or Michigan for spring tryouts and being told I've made the team. A helium balloon expands in my chest. He deserves this moment.

Before I think too hard about what I'm doing, I pull out my phone.

Three—

I backspace and start over.

Sam, I saw the news about Clemson. Congrats! I hope the moment you signed that paper was everything you dreamed of. I know you're always going to be hustling and proving yourself, and I bet by tomorrow you'll be running drills again. But I hope that at least for tonight, you're enjoying the hell out of it all. And I hope you're as proud of yourself as I am of you. Go Tigers!

I thumb the send button before I can stop myself and set my phone facedown on the side table. My hands already itch to pick it back up and see if he's responded. But I can't sit here dot-watching. He might not answer at all. Maybe he's too busy. Or maybe he doesn't want to talk to me anymore. Either way, I can't jump desperately every time my phone dings or, worse, sink lower and lower into my emotions when it stays silent.

Across the room, my eyes meet Nelly's. She's standing by the drink coolers holding two cans of LaCroix. Orange flavor, which is kinda gross but better than nothing. She holds one out to me. I take a breath, smile, and walk over to her, leaving my phone behind.

I manage not to check it again until I leave the party. He's responded, and I eagerly thumb the message open. All it says is:

Thanks ☺ And congrats on Nationals.

The energy of the party and the excitement of my squad fizzle, leaving me exhausted. I sink into the front seat of Paris's car and stare out the window as she drives me home. My phone screen stays dark. I want to open it back up, look at the message again. Make sure that's all there is. Five words and an emoji. Make sure he didn't text again and I somehow missed it. But I know he hasn't. He's said all he has to say.

I open the phone back up and skip Sam's message. Instead, I scroll down to a text Gisela's son, David, sent me a few days ago. His mom put us in touch after that meeting at the synagogue. He already has a co-organizer for the voter registration event, a youth leader from Intown Church, and to be honest, I've learned that wouldn't be the right role for me. However, they are looking for someone to help with volunteers to man the registration table. So I text David.

> If you still need a volunteer coordinator, I'm your girl. Tell me when you need me, and I'll be there.

20

ELEANOR

My feet pound the pavement of the Peachtree Park running oval. Just after sunrise, I have the place to myself. Only a few hard-core runners come out this early, especially on Sunday mornings. I like it best this way, when there's no need to dodge other runners or fight for inside track space. When I get to be alone with the slowly warming air and the still-wet grass and my thoughts. It surprises me that I crave the head space running gives me, when I felt the exact opposite last summer. But I need it. I run every day, even though cheer practices are done for the year.

Forever, I remind myself. *High school cheerleading is over.*

Not having practice to rush off to every day of the week, not having the goal of Nationals to strive toward, has left me weightless. I feel like an astronaut floating around in zero gravity, swimming through the air and knocking into things by accident.

Tryouts for the Georgia State squad will happen in a few weeks. For the first time since I was little, I'm nervous for them. I genuinely don't know if I'll make it. I've never not known how I stack up against the other girls at a tryout. College will be different. Unknown competition. Unknown coach. First time cheering without Nelly. First time trying out since the concussions. I guess, in a way, I'm an unknown, too, after all the things that have happened this year.

Most of the time, I feel okay about the fact that I might not make the team. But sometimes, the thought of failing sets my skin on fire, makes me want to go straight outside to practice stunts. Makes me want to log on to that cheer site Nelly used to obsesses over and spiral down an online rabbit hole, trying to figure out which girls are going to Georgia State. I avoid that with stern reminders that I can only control myself and how I prepare. I'm keeping in shape and practicing with Paris and some of the other girls who also plan to try out for their college teams.

I've also started going on the Georgia State website and researching other activities I might want to participate in. I've started making other plans. It's weird, but that stops the spiral better than anything else.

I'm so lost in my own head that I don't notice him until he's running beside me. Most runners are solitary types, and I assume whoever it is will toss me a wave and keep to themself. But a body pulls up next to me and stays. I glance over and miss my next step. He looks just like he did at the end of last summer, when running this oval was our thing. He wears a black Dri-FIT shirt with a Clemson logo on the breast. He's already stepped into his future, and it's secure. I feel a stinging flash of jealousy.

"Been a while since I saw you out here, Greenberg," Three says.

"Could say the same to you," I huff, sounding far more winded than he does. I could chalk that up to the fact that I've been running for thirty minutes already. But sweat drips down his neck. This is his first lap around the oval, and it's not that hot yet, which means he ran here. I shake my head. Of course.

"Busy couple of months."

We run side by side for a few minutes, Three adjusting his pace to match mine. I should say something, but I don't know what. I exhausted all the words I had for him back in February, and we haven't spoken since. I don't know if my efforts to avoid him were just one hundred percent successful or if he was avoiding me too.

"Hey, y'all killed it at your competition, by the way. Never did get a chance to tell you that. Bull showed me some video. You're badasses."

He's seen us cheer on the sidelines of his games for years. I wonder why it took him seeing it on video to notice. "Thanks."

A brief frown crosses his face. "Wanna throw it back and do some Tabata training?"

Oh god, I remember those brutal drills. I'm tempted to say no. But they were great for my stamina, and it's been a while since I exercised that hard. With tryouts coming up, I could use the push. Three was always good at pushing my workouts in a positive direction. I nod.

By the time we've completed the first set of intervals, I've time-traveled to last fall, when hanging out with Three was easy and fun. When he reminded me of the strength I thought the concussions had stolen from me permanently. Inside of thirty minutes, I'm back in that place, and it feels good. Sturdy. Powerful. And this time, Three taps out first.

"Want some water?"

We collapse on a bench as he digs two huge Clemson-branded sports bottles out of his bag. I raise my eyebrows.

"They gave me a bunch of stuff," he says with a sheepish smile. "I'm just trying to put it to good use."

"I'm not sure I should take that. Orange clashes terribly with this shade of blue."

He glances at my sweat-soaked Georgia State T-shirt. "Gonna be weird seeing you on someone else's sidelines next year."

"I don't know if I'll be on the sidelines. Not all of us signed commitment letters back in February."

"You will be."

"What makes you so sure?"

"Do you want it?"

I hesitate. I haven't talked about how much I want it with anyone. I try not to think about it too directly. "Yeah. I want it."

He nods. "Then you'll get it."

His certainty floods through me, warming my insides, which isn't really necessary, since I'm still overheated from the workout. *Definitely from the workout,* I tell myself. *Not from his attention.* I went down that path once already. I'm not foolish enough it do it again.

I accept the water bottle. "I should be grateful you're sharing your hideous orange bottles instead of stealing mine. All it took was some free Clemson gear, huh? You walk around with these all the time, ready to hand out water to unprepared surprise workout buddies?"

"Nah," he says, draping his arm across the back of the bench and looking off toward the oval. "Just when I'm hoping to run into you."

I choke. Water dribbles over my chin and onto my shirt. Casual as anything, he pounds on my back until I stop spluttering. "What?" I say.

"I wanted to ask you something. I thought maybe I'd get you in a good mood with all those endorphins."

My hand freezes in the act of wiping off my mouth. "What do you need me in a good mood for?"

"Are you going to prom?"

I wish I could say I don't float right off the ground when he says the word *prom*. But that would be a lie. I'm immediately a ball of pulsating hope that he's about to ask me. Which I should not be. Cannot be. Didn't I just tell myself I've seen this movie already and know how it ends?

"Cuz Bull and Paris and a bunch of people are getting limos and all that stuff. Marisol and Londie, too. Paris didn't know what your plans were. I asked—I don't know if she was just trying to spare my feelings or if she was trying to keep me away from you. But I figure we can't miss the senior prom thing, right? It's once in a lifetime."

Three has never once babbled. Probably not in his life. And yet, he's rambling on right now. About going to prom. With me.

No, wait—with a group of friends, which includes Bull. Which reminds me of the harsh words he said to me. Harsh, but real and right. I'm not going to assume this invitation is what I want it to be. I have to *ask*.

"Three, are you asking me to prom?" My palms are sweating, and it's not from the workout.

"Man, that must've been a weak effort if you couldn't even tell."

The urge to laugh it off swells like a tidal wave. It would be easier to tease back and live with the ambiguity. I push that desire into a box, clear my throat, and say firmly, "I feel like I do need to be clear, though." I wind my fingers into the hem of my shirt and turn sideways on the bench to look at him. "Is this a group thing? Or are you asking me as your date?"

"Come on. As my date."

"You can't blame me for being surprised. We haven't spoken in months. The last time I texted, your response… It didn't exactly leave me thinking the next logical step was that we'd go to prom together."

"Leni—"

"No, Three. I don't want to be one of those girls who chases you." My mouth curls around my next words, hating that this term gets applied to anyone ever. But I say it all the same. "The locker-room lice."

"You're not," he says. I shrug, but he sets a hand on my arm and leans close. "You never were. Look, I'm sorry about how things went. I never meant for my family to get in the way of whatever was going on between us. I was under a lot of pressure, and I didn't handle it very well. I admit I kinda wanted to have my cake and eat it too. I liked when things were easy between us, and I enjoyed the attention."

"Yeah. You said and did some really hurtful things, Three. But I'm not trying to say it was all your fault. That would be unfair. You didn't handle it well, but I had a hard time understanding everything that was going on with you. I'm sorry I pushed."

"Sorry I walked. I've never wanted a reversed call so bad in my life so I could redo that play. I have to ask one more time. You think you might wanna go to prom with me after all, or should I just recognize that I've fumbled the ball in my own end zone and move on?"

"I don't want to be the girl who's convenient."

"Believe me, the last thing you are is convenient."

I can't stop the laugh that bursts from me. That didn't sound smooth and practiced, like the flirtatious comments he used to make. It sounded like an admission. A confession that hurt a little bit on the way out. And it's enough to convince me.

"Okay, Three. I'll go to prom with you."

―――――――

The last big event to get through before prom is the Letterman Banquet honoring athletes.

It's basically an homage to Three, considering all the records he broke this year. He walks the stage—tastefully decorated by Mrs. Irons with flowers and a blue-and-green balloon arch—to accept awards so often, they stop sending him back to his seat and let him stay on the dais. His family commandeers two tables up front, and they're filled with his parents, his brothers, and their families—even Ray, who stands and cheers for our very own superstar as loud as anyone.

I don't go over to say hello. Three and I might be on better terms, but I doubt that extends to his family, and I don't have the energy for them right now. Today has been a day of good vibes, and I'm not going to ruin that with an encounter with Three's mother.

Across the room, Nelly hugs her favorite person in the school, Ms. Robertson, while Mr. and Mrs. Irons shake hands with the coaches. I slink back. Yet another set of parents I'm avoiding. I haven't spent much time around the Ironses since her suspension. It would be easier to disappear into a wall than figure out what to say to them, or anyone else here. This kind of thing has always been Nelly's show.

One of the few freshmen to make the squad this year, Carolina, squeezes through the crowd and takes a leap at me. I catch her and anchor myself so we don't topple to the ground.

"Maybe you should have been a base," she jokes.

"No, I was built to fly." I smile and give her a hug. "Just like you." After practices ended for the season, I started working with her on some stunts. She's a natural talent but lacks confidence. I have a feeling it'll come.

"I just wanted to say thanks for all the hours you spent throwing me into the air on that gymnastics mat in your backyard. I have no idea how I'm going to make the team without your help next year. But maybe I can come watch you cheer at Georgia State sometime? Maybe you can show me your dorm room and stuff too?"

The instinct to brush off her certainty overwhelms me, just like it did with Three and everyone else who has asked about the future of my cheer career. But I can't drag Carolina down like that. She deserves to hear me being confident about my chances, just like I want her to be confident about hers. Honestly, maybe I deserve to hear some of that from myself.

"I'd like that, Carolina," I say. "I'm going to miss you."

She pulls me in for another tight, fast embrace. Before I'm even able to hug her back, she's gone. I watch her disappear into the crowd, blinking rapidly to keep my tears from falling. And that's when I see Nelly standing a few feet away. I smile timidly at her.

"She's my favorite."

She clicks her tongue against her front teeth. "You're not supposed to have favorites."

"I can't help myself."

"You never could," she says. But there's laughter in her voice. She edges closer, and for a minute, we watch the party together. "So, are you going to try to cheer next year?"

"Yes. Much to my parents'—" I stop short. It's an easy refrain to fall back on, that they're dismayed, but it's not necessarily true. They didn't argue when I announced I'd be trying out. At first, they just seemed relieved when I got into Georgia State, and I had a whole speech prepared.

"I'm going to stop trying to convince you to love this

as much as I do," I said. "I know you never will. I just need you to trust me to make my own choices."

My mom wrapped her arms around me. "We do. And we promise to support your choices, including cheer. As long as you promise to remember that you're more than your squad, more than cheering, even when it's hard, okay?"

That seemed like a reasonable promise to make, so I did.

I turn back to Nelly. "Anyway. Are you?"

She shakes her head. "I'm not deciding on any of my extracurriculars until I get to Penn and see what's in store."

I blink. This is a whole new Nelly—I've never known her to do anything big without a plan. My heart pinches to think I didn't see the evolution that brought her here.

"I miss you," I blurt. I just want her to know.

Her chest rises and falls in a heavy sigh. "Me too."

But. There is definitely a *but.* She doesn't need to say it. I know. It's there for me too. We're not the same. Too much has happened this year. We can't go back to the friendship we had before. I crave it anyway.

"So, are you all ready for prom?" No doubt she's had her dress for weeks and a limo and dinner reservations all planned. I wonder if she's going with the group of unattached cheerleaders or if she's found a date.

"I'm not going."

"What?"

"My mom's sorority chapter is putting on a legacies weekend for rising college freshman," she says.

"What does that involve?"

"I don't know, actually. I think it's to prepare us for what to expect when school starts in the fall. But Alana went when it was her turn, and she said it was really helpful. Plus, some very prestigious alumni are speaking."

That sounds like more fun for Nelly than prom would be. "Cool. I'm glad you're doing that, even though prom won't be the same without you."

She glances over at me and holds my gaze for a long minute. "Well, if you don't already have a dress, I could go shopping with you."

My breath catches. "Really?"

"It's the least I could do. Without me, who knows what kind of strange cocktail attire you'd pick out for yourself."

"I'd like that a lot," I say with a laugh. She's not wrong. One week away from prom, and I've already returned four dresses I picked out online, tried on, and then regretted. "You know, if you're looking for other things to keep you busy now that cheer is done, I'm helping coordinate volunteers for a voter registration drive at the Intown Church college fair. I could use your masterful organizational skills."

Nelly considers this for a moment with a reluctant look on her face. "I can't say I have time for all that, but I'm happy to take a volunteer shift."

That's fair. It's honestly more than I hoped for. "I'll send you the schedule."

She reaches over and gives my arm a quick squeeze before joining her parents to take pictures with the awards she won.

The dress Nelly helps me pick out is perfect. It's pale blue with a tulle skirt, spaghetti straps, and a crystal-embellished bodice that sparkles whenever the light hits it. Bull, whose vest matches Paris's pink halter-neck two-piece number, tried to convince Three he should match me too. He refused. He's still the hottest guy at the prom in a slim-cut classic tuxedo with a black shirt and a bow tie. All eyes are on him most of the night. I can't even be annoyed about it, considering I'm having a hard time looking away myself. We're not prom king and queen—that honor goes to Bull and Paris—but the attention he commands makes it hard not to feel like I'm on the arm of royalty anyway. I can't even imagine what life is going to be like for him next year, when he's a fixture on Saturday-afternoon television.

"Come on," I say as the night begins to wind down. "We haven't gotten our picture taken yet."

"Those cheesy things?" he complains, but he lets me pull him into the line without any resistance.

We line up behind Marisol, who is dressed in a slim-cut

gray pinstripe suit, and Londie, who wears a gray-lavender goddess-style gown that accentuates her height.

"Cute necklace," I say, catching sight of the half-broken heart charm dangling from a silver chain around Londie's neck. It also bears half a rainbow and the word *forever*. Marisol grins and pulls the *together* half of the necklace from beneath her collar. I guess they're going to do the long-distance thing in college after all.

I glance at Three and then shiver, rubbing my hands briskly over my arms to get rid of the goose bumps. *Not going there, Leni.*

"You know, I was thinking," Three says after Londie and Marisol step forward for their turn with the photographer. "When you get to school next year, you should call my aunt. Couldn't hurt to have a department head checking for you now and again."

"You'd be okay with that?"

He shrugs, but it's not as casual as he's obviously trying to make it. "It's cool. She liked you. I think you two would get along real well."

I smile and decide not to tell him that the first thing I did when I got my acceptance letter was email her. Or that she emailed back a few minutes later, telling me she expected me not only to stay in touch but to show up to her club meetings and take a class with her. The fact that he suggested it is enough.

When it's our turn with the photographer and his predictably cheesy fabric backdrop of painted twinkle lights, we agree to the very *very* cheesy traditional pose. Three stands behind me and slides his hands over my hips. I shiver. I can't help it.

"You know what else I was thinking?" His mouth is so close, I can feel his lips brush my cheek. "You should come to a game at Clemson, see me play. It's only a couple hours up the road."

"Oh yeah? And what if it conflicts with my schedule? I might be traveling with the team, you know."

He presses closer. "True."

"Maybe you should come see me cheer. It's only a couple hours up the road, after all."

Laughter rumbles through his chest, and the touch of his lips against my skin is deliberate now. "I'll have to see about making that happen, Greenberg."

It probably won't work out, and we both know it. The demands on our time will never allow it. In a few months at most, we'll have moved on. I wait for the wave of melancholy I felt last fall when he stopped talking to me, but it doesn't come. This night is undoubtedly the grand finale for Three and me, so I'm going to enjoy it.

We leave the photo booth hand in hand and don't let go for the rest of the night.

21

CHANEL

"This is going to be great for you," Mom says softly as she helps me pack. We stand side by side, folding clothes and placing them in my luggage. It's nice. The fresh scent of the laundry beads fills the room with a perfect amount of lavender. The sun bursts through my curtains, shining on my bed. When the last dress is folded, my mom heads toward her room. "I'll be right back."

I'm so excited to be headed to this retreat. It's the most coveted event for legacy students of my mom's sorority chapter. Attending this event before heading off to Penn is exactly what I need to meet like-minded individuals. While I'm waiting for Mom to get back, I pack my toiletries and my makeup. There's not enough space in the two cosmetics bags I have, so I rustle through the junk drawer of my dresser and find my faithful old flowered one. A few months ago, it would have been packed with all the things

I needed to self-medicate. Now it's empty. I've washed it twice, and it also smells of lavender. I load the leftover toiletries into it and place all three bags neatly inside the front pocket of my suitcase.

My mom is almost floating as she walks back into my room. She reveals a small, iridescent taffeta satchel. Inside are her cotillion pearls, the ones that have been in my family since the mid-1800s. They belonged to my great-great-great-grandmother, Cecile. They were given to her by a wealthy plantation owner who was so smitten with her that he freed her and her children. Women in my family have been presented with this necklace for nearly two centuries now, usually for huge occasions—weddings, graduations, the birth of a child. My mom loves to tell the story of my grandmother placing them around her neck for the AME debutante ball. My mother has worn them only one other time since then: her wedding day. I have been instructed for as long as I can remember on how to maintain them. One of the first rules is that they cannot not be worn daily, not if they are to be preserved for the next generation.

My mom's hand drifts down like a feather in the wind as she places the bag gently on top of the cashmere sweater in my suitcase. She looks over at me with a warm smile and says, "This is the final touch I think you need for the breakfast."

I don't even attempt to fight back my tears as I wrap

my arms around my mother and squeeze her tight. The Ivy and Pearls scholarship breakfast, which is so important to my mom that it influenced her company's name, is the most elite event of the weekend. Sometimes, the sorority president and the most esteemed sorors attend and hand out thousands of dollars' worth of scholarships to only the most deserving students. Presenting your best self at this event is critical. After the year I've had, I don't expect to hear my name called. I do, however, want to look amazing as I clap for the other girls.

"This is your chance to show the world the Chanel I know," Mom says while fighting back tears of her own. I give her a nod, and in that moment, I feel hope again.

The entire weekend takes place at the Savannah Four Seasons, which is appointed with glittering antique decor. I can't help but be grateful that I get to be here. This feels like the perfect setting to start finding my voice, like Marisol and I have been talking about. As an icebreaker on the first evening, they divide us into groups to solve a problem by brainstorming a plausible real-world solution. I take the initiative and suggest we each tackle the problem on our own and then see which solutions connect and work. I strategically have the other girls in my group start presenting at a place in the circle that means I'll get to go last. I want to listen. I want to hear what they have to say. I sit and digest as each person speaks and get completely lost in their words. These girls are all smart and capable. I notice how well put together they all are. There does appear to be an unspoken uniform—cardigan, blouse, pearls for both the ears and neck, knee-length skirt or slacks, and a charm bracelet for splash. Every suggestion is smart, efficient, original, and peppered with wit. The conversation is orderly and respectful as we discuss everyone's ideas and come up with a plan. We jot down some notes, and then Makayah and I volunteer to go to the crafts station to get some supplies for our presentation.

"I've been looking forward to meeting you," she says.

"Oh, really?"

"Yeah. You've been a hot topic in the legacy group."

"What's that?"

"It's an IG group for AKA legacies."

The last time I was in something like that, the YVP Facebook group, it soured pretty fast. I don't know if I want to be in another. But her next words make me reconsider.

"We're proud of you, sis. Jacked up how you got railroaded, though. Grapevine says you got suspended, and all those white girls on your team walked away free."

Just when I was feeling good, my saga continues.

"Yeah. I'm trying to move past it now, though. I'm focusing on some other community projects."

294

"Oh, I know. We see you out there, doing it for the culture. Anyway, seems to us like you had a stellar year. I'll add you to the group. You have fans."

"Cool, thanks." It's funny how different things look from the outside. I must admit, it feels good to know my highlights reel is viewed positively in some circles. I didn't expect that.

We volunteer to present first, and it goes off without a hitch. The pleased faces of the organizers and the impressed looks of our fellow students are invigorating. For the rest of the day, our group moves as a unit, and it seems like the beginning stage of some really great friendships. No one else in my group is attending Penn, but a few of us will be in the same region, and since we all plan on pledging, I'm going to make certain we keep in touch.

———————

By the scholarship breakfast the following morning, Makayah has added me to the legacy group. I scroll for a little while, dreading what I might see, yet hopeful the vibe she gave me was authentic and I'll find a few positive phrases attached to my name.

> Next-level female Cody Knight. It's about time the ladies took the movement back, Rosa Parks–style. We see you, Ms. Chanel.

I commend my future soror—if we don't stand for us, who will? Chanel Irons for president.

Looks like Chanel Irons will be the next Barack Obama. Anyone know if she's straight? I'm here for being her Michelle. We can un-hetero that White House together.

Who's gonna check Ms. Chanel? Nobody, that's who. Periodt! **#blackgirlmagic #blackgirlsrock**

There are so many comments like these. So, so many. I hope the person in the room next to mine doesn't think there's something wrong with me, because I can't stop the joyous laughter mixed with tears that has taken me over. Wearing my family pearls adds to the cloud I'm on. I feel like a new me. Sitting at the table with my new friends is the perfect end to this amazing weekend.

And yet, it also makes me think of Leni. I can't believe I'm not texting her updates every few minutes during such a momentous occasion. I've always been taught that relationships may be seasonal, but I thought Leni and I would be friends our whole lives. I'm glad I'm going to volunteer with her at the voter registration table, but I also know that once I go away to school, the cracks between us will widen. And I've accepted it.

A waiter removes the bread plate from in front of me and replaces it with my breakfast entree. At that very moment, there's the clink of a glass, and the national sorority secretary gives a welcome address to start the program. She's a member of this chapter, which is how she was able to get the national president to attend as a guest. As they call the names of the scholarship recipients, I clap with pride for all of these brilliant young ladies, loudest for my newfound sisters at my table. Then she appears: the president of the sorority, in all of her profound regality, to present the scholarship everyone is hoping for. She captivates the audience with her words about service, dignity, and legacy.

"Here at the seventy-eighth annual Ivy and Pearls scholarship breakfast, I'm proud to present the Crown Legacy Award for exemplifying excellence through sustainable service to Chanel Irons."

I fall back in my chair. *She said my name!* My legs feel like putty as I walk toward the podium. I can hardly hold myself up. The crowd is full of smiling faces, and they give me a standing ovation. I didn't prepare a speech. I never imagined I was in the running.

"Oh my word," I say. "Thank you to the committee and the community. I didn't expect this. Where I live, I am celebrated only by a few of my peers—my cheer team, predominately. To most others, I'm a blight on my community's good name. After spending this weekend with you exceptional women, I've learned something. We may be spread out, women like us—strong, brown, and determined—but we are here in this world. We're making dents in the spaces we're in, not knowing that we have our own cheerleaders around the country who are taking on the same fights and rooting for us to win together. That's the beauty of this sorority. It's a brave space for us to support one another. As I take this award home, I know I'm taking the strength of you all with me."

And that's exactly what I need.

ACKNOWLEDGMENTS

As usual, we have a long and spectacular list of people to thank. We're grateful to have this much support in an endeavor like writing which can often be so solitary. If we've forgotten anyone here, please charge it to our heads and not our hearts.

First, we have to thank the entire Sourcebooks family. We're overwhelmed by how ardently you've championed us and helped us share our stories with the world. You're our ride or die forever. We especially want to thank Dominique Raccah, Todd Stocke, Steve Geck, Cassie Gutman, Zeina Elhanbaly, Lizzie Lewandowski, Beth Oleniczak, Margaret Coffee, Caitlin Lawler, Stefani Sloma, Sarah Kasman, Tiffany Schulz, Mallory Hyde, Valerie Pierce, Danielle McNaughton, Nicole Hower, Jordan Kost, and Sarah Cardillo. We're indebted to you also for this novel's beautiful cover, drawn by the talented Adriana Bellet.

We consulted with a number of expert and sensitivity readers to inform the experiences described in the book. We appreciate your kind and insightful guidance more than we can ever express. Thanks to: our cheer insider, Liz Shah; the real Dr. Ratcliff, for his help understanding concussion effects; the real Rabbi David Spinrad, for being a great model of social justice oriented clergy; our Divine Nine beta readers, Courtney Jones and Reece Odum; Michelle Rinke, for helping us do our best to sensitively render Nelly's mental health journey; and, of course, e.e. Charlton-Trujillo and Arlondie Washington. Readers, please know that any mistakes in the rendering of the story are on us and not them.

We also want to thank our agents, Tracey and Josh Adams, and our film agent, Stephen Moore, for midwifing *Why We Fly* into the world of books and movies. We're so excited to work with our fabulous production partners, Radar Productions and Prominent Pictures, especially Autumn Bailey-Ford. We're grateful to you for including us in the process and taking such care with our story. We adore you.

We'd also like to add the following thanks:

From Kim:

I want to acknowledge my mom, Lula, and my son, Drake, who freely share me with the world without complaint, and Ikeeah, who doubles as my favorite niece and awe-inspiring assistant, who keeps my head on straight.

I also want to thank my manager and partner, Duprano, my attorney, Uwonda Carter Scott, and my Warner family, Nik and Lee, who always champion my storytelling.

From Gilly:

A hundred million thanks to my family, which has shown up for me at every point and in every manner—from providing words of encouragement to proofreading to watching my kids so I can run around the country living my bookish dream. Mom, Dad, Stacey, Noam, Nadav, and Shalev, you're the very best part of it all, and I couldn't do any of this without you. I also wouldn't want to do any of this without all of the writer friends who hold me down and lift me up, especially Maryann Dabkowski and Rachael Allen.

ABOUT THE AUTHORS

 Kimberly Jones is the former manager of the bookstore Little Shop of Stories and currently works in the entertainment industry. She's also an activist, well-known for her viral video "How Can We Win." Visit her at kimjoneswrites.com.

Gilly Segal grew up in Florida before she left home to attend the University of Pennsylvania, Hebrew University, and Emory School of Law. She is currently chief legal officer for an advertising agency. Visit her at gillysegal.com.